# TV
# MAN

# TV MAN

## Rodrick Bradley

Holt, Rinehart and Winston    New York

Copyright © 1981 by Rodrick Bradley

Published by Holt, Rinehart and Winston,
383 Madison Avenue, New York, New York 10017.

Published simultaneously in Canada by Holt, Rinehart and
Winston of Canada, Limited.

Library of Congress Cataloging in Publication Data

Bradley, Rodrick.
TV man.

I. Title.
PZ4.B7999Tad    [PS3552.T2298]    813'.54    80-13326

ISBN Hardcover: 0-03-056701-7
ISBN Paperback: 0-03-057791-8
First Edition

Cover photograph by Rodrick Bradley

Designer: Constance T. Doyle

Printed in the United States of America
1 3 5 7 9 10 8 6 4 2

To the residents of the Palms Hilton
and all of those who live in rented rooms

*"Every act of rebelling expresses a nostalgia for innocence."*

—*Albert Camus*

A hot wind blew him up the boulevard in a daze, the air impelling him toward the mustard-yellow letters that marched gigantically across the roof of a low brick warehouse: MEANY'S TV—LARGEST IN THE WEST.

The wind slapped a sheet of yellowed newsprint against the back of his legs. He tore it away and watched the dead headlines sail around the edge of the building. The air ripped at his lungs and his nostrils burned, but despite the stifling heat he took three quick strides and made a graceful leap onto the loading dock. He paused at a smudgy gray door, breathless with the effort of his jump. Bright spots swam in his eyes. Jesus, he thought. It's my birthday.

He stood hesitant at the door, paralyzed by conflicting waves of emotion. His eyes stung. It was just the filthy air, he told himself. He looked over the row of red vans emblazoned with Meany's emblem: a comic doctor holding a stethoscope to an anthropomorphic television set with its tongue hanging out. His own spot was empty: the van had broken down for the third time that week. He knew Hazard was not going to see it as just bad luck. But there was no way to avoid him. He had to pick up his check.

He pushed open the door, and for a moment he saw nothing but a great darkness. He sensed a vague hum, the breath of old television sets, and a febrile gnawing in the dead air. Then his vision took in the stripe of intense light at the far end of the darkness: the glassed office that overlooked the mammoth workroom. He started toward the light, his steps echoing between tables spread with the hulks of disemboweled sets. They smelled: a subtle but piquant electronic decay. At first the fact that something so inert could have such a strong scent had intrigued him, but now he hated it. The smell made him queasy, and seemed to follow him everywhere.

The rows of tables ended and he passed through corridors of refurbished sets waiting for auction, most of them dark, but a few silently displaying whatever picture was fed out of the airwaves. A surgeon of television sets. That's what he'd ended up, out of no particular desire, but out of listlessness. Or fate. Because the army had determined his aptitude and sent him to school and told him to fix radios and radar and for two years he'd done it, not particularly minding, at times even liking it: like finding a missing piece in a jigsaw puzzle. He was good at it, good at anything he really put his mind to. But lately his mind wandered. Broken circuits, he thought, too much dope and something else. The smell. Maybe he was just allergic to the smell.

"Keller? Is that you?"

The voice startled him, booming over the intercom.

"Welcome back, soldier."

Harry glanced up at the office and saw him sitting at his desk, microphone in hand, utterly secure, the commander of a vessel. He could see the man's mouth move before the sound reached him.

"What you waiting for, Harry? Come up and get your check."

He hesitated a moment in futile defiance. A fire rose in his belly, spread through his chest. He started up the stairs, each step sapping his strength, sweat stinging his eyes. He counted the steps, already knowing how many there were. The thirteenth step took him into the office.

"Harold Keller," the man said as if recalling a name with

affectionate nostalgia. The chair swung and presented the beaming face. Everything about it was quite perfect: an easy handsome face without a crack to wedge his hatred in.

"Well, Harry," the man said with that soft intonation that made Harry think of slime. "I hear you had another breakdown—"

The quip came without premeditation: "Not yet, Mr. Hazard. A little floating anxiety, a crisis of confidence, but the breakdown—"

"Is this supposed to be a joke, Harry? You stoned or what?"

"I been stoned all right," he said without a trace of sarcasm.

"Yes, well," Hazard said and swiveled back to face his desk, leaving Harry to look down on the broad shoulders, the white shirt still crisp, the sleek waves of hair so light it was almost silver, not too long, not too short. "I like you, Harry, but I get the feeling it isn't mutual."

Harry shifted back and forth on his feet watching the man shuffle through a dozen unclaimed payroll checks.

"The point is, Harry, you haven't been toeing the line. Haven't made the quotas for weeks. A lot of no-shows and repeat calls. Now if you don't want the job, that's your business. You do what you got to do, and I do what I got to, okay?"

The man swung back around and offered Harry his hand. Harry had seen the gesture before: it was a request for complicity with Hazard's code of employee subordination. Harry stared: the man's hand seemed to leap in proportions, like a trick.

"How about my check?"

"Sure, Harry, sure." The gigantic hand moved. The check rattled in his face.

"I'll have to cash it for you, Harry."

"Shit, it isn't fair," Harry said.

"Fair is what you make it, Harry. I'm doing you a favor."

[ 5 ]

The man stood, put his arm over Harry's shoulder, and bent his face close in a show of virile intimacy. His breath smelled waxy, like lipstick, and underneath Harry caught the musk of sweat, hint of the locker room. The man's hand seemed cold and heavy; Harry wanted to shrug it off, wanted to slam his elbow into the man's gut, stand smirking as Hazard bent gasping.

"Harry, Harry, you mustn't think these things."

"I need the check, Mr. Hazard. For christ's sake, it's my birthday." The moment Harry said it, he was overwhelmed by an inexplicable feeling of remorse.

"Well, I'll be. Congratulations!" The man's voice rang with sincerity. "You should've told me earlier. Listen, I'll give you a lift to the Goosedown, buy you a drink. My god, you should've told me."

Hazard handed Harry the check. He folded it and tucked it in his pocket, moved out from under Hazard's arm. He went down the stairs, taking them fast. He veered into the men's room, flinched at the sharp scent of disinfectant.

It felt oddly comforting in his hand, the slight tremor of vacating urine, the warm softness: for a moment he was sure who he was, saw himself standing in the red surgeon coat embroidered with Meany's slogan, leaned back, eyes closed, relishing the splash against porcelain, the acrid scent, the simple pleasure of release. He was just tall enough and thin enough to appear slightly awkward when at rest, an impression that was refuted by the grace of his movements. His face also contained elements of paradox: it was not pretty, but roughly handsome in a homey boyish way so he was continually being mistaken for someone a decade younger. Yet he was aware of the deepening lines settling around his eyes. His eyes were exceptional, deep-set, vibrant green, alive. He thought they were too close, and found himself embarrassed by their intensity. Yet he meant no harm. In fact his posture was generally stooped forward in friendly benediction and interest, a posture that more successfully than he knew disguised any feelings of anger, frustration, or need. In a way he was too well hidden, for even when he was genuinely enraged, people seemed to find his anger almost comic.

"Harry . . ." Hazard's voice burst over the intercom. "I almost forgot to mention you got an opportunity to be on call this weekend, so if you're squeezed . . . anyway, happy birthday, soldier. I'll be waiting on the dock."

Katherine Ann Kruse, known as Kitty, walked up the alley holding her purse against her face to protect herself from windblown debris. She came to a red enameled door marked in carelessly scrawled yellow letters: ARTISTS' ENTRANCE, and bracing her back against it, shoved it open. The stink of stale alcohol stirred in her a brief foreboding, but at least the interior air was cool and its filth different from the filth outside. She entered the dressing room and twisted on a single sixty-watt bulb stuck over a peeling mirror. She took off a pair of blue-lensed glasses and sat in the rickety wooden folding chair before a Formica-topped table and was reminded of Sunday school: she saw the little circle of chairs, the idealized portraits of the Savior, heard the voice of her mother lapping over the scrubbed rosy faces, smelled again the lilacs she had carried along the neat suburban streets of Urbana, Illinois, to set atop the piano. The memory annoyed her, for it had no logic, no significance other than to remind her she wasn't getting younger. She leaned toward the mirror and her hands moved over her face with the various brushes, pomades, powders, moving too quickly, as if somehow to arrest the flight of all lost time. She pushed the pencil across the thin brows, arching them high into her forehead. The pencil broke and she slammed it down, hissing.

"Temper, temper." A ravaged velveteen curtain drew

aside and a woman stepped out draped in diaphanous black, a long mane of blond curls running to her bared breasts that were of such perfect symmetry as to be of dubious authenticity.

"You know, Veronica," Kitty said whining.

"What, honey?"

"I wish you'd stop calling me honey."

Veronica laughed softly and shook her head, then eased her hands onto the younger woman's shoulders, her fingers working at the tightened muscles.

"Relax. You just got to relax or you'll wear yourself to a frazzle before you're thirty."

"If you don't mind I'll decide how to wear myself out."

Veronica shrugged. "Suit yourself."

Kitty drew herself away from the woman's hands, and traced a swath of silver shadow over each of her pale cobalt eyes, intensifying their impression of coldness and size to the point where they appeared slightly disproportionate, as though she were perpetually astonished and simultaneously critical of everything she saw. She loved makeup, relished underscoring the theatrical qualities of her face, yet her pleasure was more formal than sensual. The last image she wanted to project was: Whore. Not a whore like Veronica, a perfect example of the type she had to compete with for the almighty bucks tossed by leering males into the beer pitcher at the edge of the stage when she should have been floating through a *pas de deux* with Nureyev—or if not the star himself, some up-and-coming male dancer of similar power and grace. For really, Kitty, you do have it, she told herself, if you'd only got the breaks.

Veronica sighed: "Isn't life a damn gas?"

Kitty didn't say anything. There was a silence and the two women let their eyes meet in the mirror. The jukebox began to play, the sound coming through the walls as a thumping bass resonance with occasional overtones of agonized voice speaking of love and its betrayal, signaling to the women they would soon have to appear on the small oval stage.

"You never did tell me if you scored," Veronica said.

Kitty reached under the table, pulled up a handmade leather purse, and took from it a clear plastic envelope. She opened it, and the blond woman interrupted her makeup to stick her nose in: she inhaled deeply, exaggerated her pleasure with raised eyebrows. Kitty pulled out a portion of the dark dried vegetation sticky with resin, and rolled it into a cigarette.

Their mouths left red smudges on the paper; now and then their fingers would touch, even linger in the touch, finding a purchase on the shortening stub. There was a pause in the thumping of the jukebox, then a new song asserted itself and with it came a sense of the growing herd of males with their virile and drunken expectations as they sat at tables below the stage, or occupied stools along the bar. They came from the twilit sidewalk through the curtain yellow with nicotine, into the darkness punctuated by pools of colored light. They came alone, sometimes in pairs or triplets, but never with women. The Goosedown Club was, as Mr. Keats the bartender said, "a pleasantly sleazy theater for the male to get his ego lushed." Mr. Keats was known as a nice man, a bit of a philosopher, and someone who could get along with a drunk. The women heard his step outside the dressing room, and his knock soft as if with gloved hand.

"My dear ladies, it's after eight o'clock," he said in singsong voice.

"It's all right, Mr. Keats. Come on in," Veronica said.

"No ladies, you better come out. The beasts are restless."

Veronica laughed: "Be out in a jiff, Mr. Keats," and still laughing turned to Kitty. "He's the only thing that makes this place tolerable."

"I guess so," Kitty said.

"My, aren't you the moody one tonight."

"Sorry."

"I thought that smoke'd cheer you up."

Kitty felt her eyes warm, and her chest tighten.

"Hey, what's up?" the woman said.

She let forth a thwarted little laugh, shaking her head. "Nothing. I'm just—maybe it's the wind. Or Los Angeles. Or—"

The woman laughed: "I know how it is, honey, but you just got to shrug it off or you'll kill yourself. I mean it isn't half-serious. It's a big game, you know?"

Kitty nodded. As much as she didn't want to, she couldn't help but admire the woman's good cheer. For a moment she experienced a disquieting impulse to embrace her, even to kiss her, the image so vivid she saw it happening; then she realized she was staring at Veronica's mouth.

"You have a beautiful face, honey," Veronica said. "You could go a long way."

"Sure," Kitty said.

"Every try modeling?"

"My hips—I'm not built right."

"Nonsense."

"They want skinny ones, like yours."

"But I got too much up top," she laughed. "Besides I got a working-class face."

"I wish mine were bigger."

"You got beauties, honey. I'm just lucky these have stayed up. Listen, you need some quick money? Is that it?"

"Sure, who doesn't?"

"No, forget it."

"Tell me."

"It's not your line."

"Tell me," Kitty said. "You don't know me that well."

"Listen, you try and get yourself together, I gotta go entertain the beasts."

The woman bent and Kitty felt the sudden press of a kiss, the hot tip of tongue—or had she dreamed it? She leaned toward the mirror searching for some trace of the woman's kiss. She found none. Then in a movement so lingering as to appear involuntary, she began to smear makeup over the glass. Muffled handclaps and male caterwauls vibrated through the walls announcing Veronica's appearance on stage.

An electric blue snake of letters burned against a pale green sky. GOOSEDOWN CLUB . . . GOOSEDOWN CLUB. Below the letters a yellow neon goose jerked its head and periodically shook a shower of white stars off its tail. The letters, full of extravagant loops and twists, seemed to leap out at him as the big car pulled to the curb and lurched to a stop.

"Hey Harry, what you waiting for?"

For a moment he'd forgot who he was with. He got out. The door thunked shut with a solid wealthy sound.

Hazard brushed aside the curtain and ushered Harry into the darkness as if leading him into his own living room, rambling on in his soft easy voice. They sat in a corner booth and ordered. The drinks arrived and were shoved across the table. She stood looking down at them, one hand on her bare hip, her face scornful. His temptation was to stare at the soft flare of her belly, inner curve of thigh, the strands of pubic curl escaping the hug of skimpy silk: but she was too fragile, too naked.

"That's two-sixty, gentlemen," she said. "Anything for the dancers is appreciated, just put it in the pitcher on stage. All we get is tips."

It was a pat speech, a weary request, almost a beg. Harry fished out his wallet and handed her three bills. When she made a token gesture to make change, he waved it off.

"Thank you, gentlemen."

As she turned to leave, Hazard caught her arm.

"Hey Kitty, what makes you so friendly tonight?"

She shrugged and again started to move away, and again was caught.

"I want you to meet my buddy Harry. Going to be a big man someday. Happens to be his birthday."

"How nice," she said and put on a smile that edged toward a sneer.

"Glad to meet you," Harry said and extended his hand across the table. She ignored it. Trying to cover his embarrassment, he quickly withdrew and combed his fingers through his hair. She was still standing there, still with that expression of barely concealed disdain. She looked so young. Except for her eyes, too cold to be young.

"You new here?" he heard himself say.

"That's right. 'Fresh meat,' as they say."

Hazard laughed with forced hilarity: "Damn, Kitty, I thought you were all innocence."

"I'm getting tough," she said.

"Taking lessons from Veronica, huh?" Hazard slapped her bottom with presumptuous jocularity. She stood with a sick grin, utterly immobile. Harry silently wished her luck, but he sensed she wouldn't be able to keep it up: it was all an act. He knew. He did it himself. When he was alone he was a great actor, but only when alone.

"You make me sick," Kitty said, and whirled to leave. Hazard lunged and flicked her rump with the back of his hand.

"Hey!" Harry said.

"She loves it," Hazard replied. "You don't understand them, Harry. She thinks she's so sophisticated, so superior, but what she wants is this." He slammed his fist into his palm in demonstration, then leaned across the table: "What you bet I can lay her tonight, huh?"

Harry didn't answer. He was watching the girl move back to the bar, and then to the curtained doorway beside the stage. She passed through the curtains, then reemerged wrapped in a heavy fur coat and leaned in the doorway smoking a cigarette, watching the other woman dance. While Harry watched Kitty, Russell Hazard was telling him in tones of exaggerated solicitude how he, Harry, had betrayed himself. Variations on an old theme. A dog-eat-dog world. You choose what you want to be. Question of mental attitude. You, Harry, have chosen to be exactly where you are.

The music ended and the stage lights were momentarily doused. There was mad applause. The lights flicked on and the blond woman stood naked with hips thrust out. Her fingers parted the dark heart-shaped hair between her thighs to reveal startling pink. She slowly inserted a finger. Harry turned away, disgusted by his own undeniable thrill. Coins rattled on the floor. Bills filled the glass beer pitcher. The room was a pandemonium of whistles and whoops. Again the lights died.

When the stage lights next came on, Kitty stood in their beams, wrapped in the fur coat, a stance of defiance. The music began. She moved with sharp precise bursts, a leg emerging in a kick, a glimpse of belly, a whirl, the coat flaring outward, then a quick withdrawal. She did not look at them, but above them into the bank of spotlights, or back at her own reflection in the mirrored wall. At first they were quiet in hushed expectation, but after the second song they grew restless, urging her to drop the coat. When their urgings had died into indifferent grumbles, she disdainfully let the coat fall. She danced on in black underwear, defying calls to reveal herself further.

"Not too meaty, is she?" Hazard said. "Except for that ass. A lot of pizazz in that ass."

Harry had thought the same himself. So how could he hit him. And if he did, he'd only get his face bashed. Besides, it wouldn't change a thing.

He watched her dance on, pretending immunity, while the men nearest the stage pummelled her with sarcastic epithets, daring her to bare herself, asking if she was too good for them. Harry could see it was all she could do not to run. He wanted to catch her eye, to tell her of his allegiance.

"Make a nice little birthday present, wouldn't she?" Hazard said, but Harry no longer heard, for he was certain the girl on stage sensed his presence in the remote dark corner. His throat ached, wanting to speak. Then, just as his mouth opened, his breath caught. He stood and watched immobile, as she eased the black silk down and let it fall to her ankles: she stood motionless, hands on hips. They yelled for her to move and she started to shake, a puppet with tangled strings.

Several men surged toward her, throwing their fists into the spotlights, casting fierce shadows over her nakedness. Harry saw bright rivulets run from her eyes. He had a twenty-dollar bill in his hand. He pushed toward the stage trying to reach the empty glass pitcher with her name. Someone threw a coin at her, then came a ferocious barrage accompanied by hissing jeers. The coins pelted her, struck the stage, rolled. She covered her face. He pushed forward and thrust his arm toward the pitcher. The bill was torn from his hand. He lunged for it. Fists hammered into his body. Warm trickles tasted coppery in his mouth. But they couldn't touch him. He was deep inside, away from them; he was going to tell her he understood—understood she was a real dancer, an artist.

He was sitting under a table. He wasn't sure how long it had lasted. Everywhere were overturned chairs, broken glass, pools of beer. The stage was empty, the quiet broken by periodic bursts of laughter and occasional curses. The bartender was extending his hand: "Come on, my man."

There was a warm sweet smell and a light too bright. A cold towel pressed his face. He shut his eyes and let them minister. They talked in hushed funereal whispers. Then he sensed the emptying of the room. Muffled music drowned muffled voices. He was alone. Or almost alone. He wanted to sit there with the towel on his face forever. He was tired, yet

[ 16 ]

his mind felt clear, the way an empty mind would feel. Then her voice filled him: "Here, try this."

A shot glass pressed into his hand. He shook his head.

"It's brandy."

He pulled the towel away. Her breath caught: "Boy, you're a mess! I hate to say it, but . . ."

At first he couldn't find her; then he saw the pale face floating above the length of fur, disembodied.

He said: "I wanted to . . ." A wash of blood ran down his throat, his voice burbled.

"I saw what happened," she said.

His arms moved toward her reflection in the mirror.

"Maybe you better see a doctor," she said. "It might be worse than Mr. Keats said. I saw a guy get killed once. Walked away just like you, then folded up right out on the sidewalk. Something happened to his insides." She snickered. "Hey, I don't mean to be depressing, I just thought, maybe you ought to get checked out."

"I'm okay," he said.

"They're pigs," she said. "Real pigs."

"They had no right," he said.

She shrugged, and stubbed out a half-finished cigarette. "You want some smoke?" she asked.

He shook his head.

"Good Colombian. Two hits and . . ." She made a swirling gesture with her hands. "But maybe you better not."

"Guess it won't hurt," he said.

He watched her mouth run across the gummed edge of the paper, her eyes avoiding his.

"Here," she said.

For a moment their fingers met, and he prolonged the touch.

"Go on, take some."

The paper stuck to his bloody lip. He pulled it away, feeling bruised skin tear. She grimaced at the dark stain, then put the cigarette gingerly to her mouth. They smoked in silence. The coat fell open and he glimpsed the hair below her belly. He wanted to fall out of the chair onto his knees, to bury his face there.

"Yeah, a bunch of pigs," she sighed.

"You know Russ?" he asked.

"The guy you were with? More than I care to," she said.

He opened his mouth to tell her about Hazard's bet; then laughter bubbled out through the blood.

"Sorry," he said and started to laugh again.

"Hey, take it easy," she said.

He nodded.

"Listen, I want to thank you," she said with sudden stiff formality, extending her hand.

He took it, bent, pressed his lips to her knuckles, all the while seeing himself and secretly laughing. Then he was on his knees.

"But I haven't told you," he heard himself saying. "I need to tell you."

"Go tell it to the moon, buster."

He felt himself fall forward. His face struck a dirty scrap of blue rug. He saw her calves flashing away from him. He smelled urine and the sweet waxiness of makeup. He got to his feet and moved through a door into a dimly lit room full of barrels and cardboard boxes. He pushed another door and was in the alley. There was no moon. He howled at a streetlamp: "Jesus god, it's my goddamn birthday, you know that?" His arms closed around emptiness and he kissed the dark.

The solder went liquid, the acrid smoke billowing up in his face. The man was asking some question, wheezy whiskey voice buzzing, but Harry wasn't there, he was thinking about the ten-year-old classic convertible he'd impulsively put a deposit on the previous day, seeing the road reflectors lick up at him, the headlights cutting a hole in the dark, the open road, dashlights low, radio rich with slow blues, the dancer named Kitty beside him, her waist delicate under his hand, her hair fluffing over his face in warm night wind. . . .

Fantasy dispersed and elation sank. Every night he'd been back, had roused up his courage and with chest tight had pushed through the dirty curtain into the jukebox-thumping darkness, but she was never there. Once he'd even managed to ask the blond woman, Veronica, who smiled, remembering him. She gave him a number and he called, palms sweating, then a sleepy male voice: *Kitty? You mean Katherine. She split a week ago. I'd like to get in touch myself. My name's Sandzone, Lee Sandzone. You might've heard of me. Listen, if you see her . . .*

The old man tapped his shoulder and held up a cheap bottle of rye: "Wanna shot?"

Harry shook his head and ran through the channels, images rattling his eyes.

"Yep, I won six hundred on that baby—you ever play the horses, fella?"

[ *19* ]

"Don't have the time."

The old man wheezed out a laugh: "Used to say that myself, young fella. Yes sir!" His laughter tumbled into a spasm of coughing. Harry packed up his tools, looked at his clipboard, checked off: Rapier Motel #14, and went out the door with the old man breathing after him: "Used to think that myself."

He knocked at #7. Waited. Knocked again. It was hot, the gray sky suffused with light. He felt soiled, not with genuine dirt, but with some vague internal grime that couldn't be cleansed. It was Saturday, another week gone, another check. He hadn't lost his job, in fact Hazard hadn't mentioned the incident at the Goosedown or his refusal to make the kickback.

A woman answered from inside: "What the hell you want?" Her voice was young, edgy, not yet awake.

"TV man."

He heard drawers open and slam; then a chain rattled, the lock turned.

"It's about time," she sneered.

He caught a glimpse of her moving away: then she was throwing her head back, her hand cupped over her mouth. She gulped from a smudgy glass on the nightstand.

"The manager of this dump said you'd be here Wednesday."

He stood in shock, mind thrashing for words, a grin tearing at the corners of his mouth.

Rapping the set with her fist, she said: "The picture comes and goes, you never know when."

He stood waiting to be recognized, unable to speak.

"You want me to leave or something?" she said.

"No. I just wanted . . ."

Her face pinched up in a frown: "Hey, buddy boy, don't get any ideas."

"Ideas?" he said in genuine confusion. "No, I just wanted to ask—"

"Listen," she said, "would you just fix the damn thing?"

She snatched up a rumpled pile of clothes from the floor and slammed the bathroom door. He heard her cursing, the curses vague in intention, but somehow directed at him; then the shower was running. He took out his tools and opened up the set.

It was a ten-minute job. He tinkered longer, frantic with excitement. Then the first doubts came: after all, he'd only seen her at the club in the pink stage light, all made up, and briefly after the fight, his brain fogged with smoke and booze. Still he was sure. He tested phrases meant to reveal his recognition, but they all seemed clumsy and stupid. He considered rifling her purse, the closet, the bureau, looking for hard evidence of her identity, but finally he rested, paralyzed not by fear of being caught so much as the fear of finding the evidence he was looking for: if he did, he would have to declare himself; if he declared himself he risked humiliation.

He kept finicking with the set. A sudden dizzy recklessness permeated his senses: she *had* recognized him, was merely pretending not, afraid of her own attractions.

"Hey, TV man—" she yelled through a crack in the bathroom door. Her voice startled him. The screwdriver slipped from his fingers. Sparks leapt, showered down, snapping and hissing. He yanked the plug.

"Jesus christ!" she said.

He stood watching the innards smolder, electric smoke filling the room.

"Now what?" she said.

He shrugged. "I'll have to call in."

"Good luck," she said.

"Yeah, thanks."

"Could you hand me my shampoo. On the dresser."

He fetched it, placed it in her extended hand, his head averted.

"Guess you'll be here awhile." The edge was gone from her voice, as if some internal switch had been thrown. The door shut and he listened for the lock, but didn't hear it. A swell of desire assaulted him, then scattered, leaving him hunched over the dead set, his breath so shallow it seemed his body of itself disdained air. He kept swallowing, his mind wandering over images of the dancer, soap sliding over her skin. He was staring at the unlocked bathroom door when she emerged in damp blue jeans, her breasts provocative shadows behind a translucent blouse, making a firm jiggle as she worked a towel over wet curls.

"That bad, huh?"

He nodded, trying not to stare. Her waist was so small, her nipples dark and erect, and she smelled nice, jesus so nice, he could feel his knees go all watery.

"Really blew it, didn't you?" she said, her voice suddenly warm.

"Yeah, I guess so," he said.

"So don't feel bad," she said. "I blew it too. Lost my job. But you know what? I don't give a damn. In fact I'm glad."

"Yeah. That's good. A real good attitude."

"So what now?" she said.

"I'll get a color set off the truck. Like new. Nineteen inches."

"Hey, that'd be all right," she said.

She was at the mirror, primping, singing a snatch of popular song, when he returned and plugged in the new set. Lush orchestral music soared over a forties hard-boiled detective driving off in the rain, his blond sweetheart nestled against his shoulder. Harry and Kitty stood mesmerized through the final fade. With no transition, an animated bedsheet was singing the powers of a soap to get clothes cleaner than clean. He switched the channels, running violently through the afternoon serials, the interchangeable voices so monotonously intense he felt an urge to smash his fist through the screen.

"The other channel," she said. " 'As the World Turns.' "

"You're kidding."

"No," she said, and slowly sat on the bed. Her hand reached out, and without a glance away from the screen, plucked the pack of cigarettes from the nightstand. Smoke streamed from her nostrils. She flicked the ashes into the smudgy glass, again without looking.

He sat beside her in mute astonishment, watching her watch. Her face went slack and smooth as she seemed to sink into embalmed serenity. She took a long drag on her cigarette, and he felt his skin prickle. He wanted to warn her, but there were no words. Besides, he might frighten her: she would think he was mad—and perhaps be right. Then his mouth opened and words came soft and rapid, pitched with nervous energy: "You're a terrific dancer," he said and at once regretted it.

But there was no danger. She hadn't heard. He moved closer, close enough so his thigh touched hers. It was all he could do to keep his breath still. He stared at her face: the full mouth, the eyes that were a little too large and pale, innocent eyes, he thought, or crazy, or both—maybe you couldn't be one without the other. Her brow furrowed in response to some savage argument on the screen. His breath ruffled the brown curls. He pushed a finger into her hair, opened a curl, and saw a large gold earring.

"Hey," she said.

"Guess I'll go," he said and stood abruptly. He remained standing, looking down in abject perplexity, ready to bolt, yet wanting to declare himself.

"Okay, thanks," she said, as the orchestral theme bubbled over the planet Earth turning slowly in the void.

"You're a terrific dancer," he repeated.

"Don't forget your tools," she said.

"You're really terrific. Just wanted to tell you."

Then she realized what he was saying: "Hey, what is this?"

"I saw you at the club."

"Oh yeah?"

"My name's Harry, remember?"

Her eyes narrowed, her face went rigid: "Yeah. I didn't recognize—you were pretty messed up."

"I'm fine," he said.

"I'm glad."

"You're really a terrific dancer, an artist."

"Thanks."

"I tried to call you. Some guy answered."

"Lee?"

He nodded. She hissed and stubbed out her cigarette: "What'd that fucker tell you? Excuse the language, but some guys are plain pricks, you know?"

He watched her pace back and forth, her hands fluttering as if she wasn't sure what to do with them: first they were on her face, then hugging her arms, then clutching the back of her neck.

"All he said is he wanted to get in touch."

"Yeah, in touch is right." Her eyes refused to look at him for more than an instant. She picked up another cigarette and struck the match repeatedly trying to get it to light.

"Listen, I thought maybe you'd like to go out, get something to eat somewhere, I know a nice little Chinese place . . ." His voice sounded rehearsed, not quite convincing. But as soon as he spoke her erratic flight around the room was arrested midstep. She turned to face him. She smiled. For a moment he thought she was going to assent, perhaps even embrace him.

"No thanks," she said.

"But why?"

She snickered. "Listen, you're real nice and all, but I'm tied up right now. In fact I got an audition in about an hour, so I think you better split."

"But I'd like to—"

"Right now, my friend. Right now, okay?"

He caught a warm animal scent and he knew it was her. Maybe it was the scent that drew him; but he couldn't touch her. No, if he touched her now she would never forgive him.

"Damn it," he said. "I'm not like them. I care about you." As soon as he said it, he felt foolish and was certain she would laugh.

"Listen, I think you better go, please, right now."

"I've got plans," he said.

"Sure, but leave me out. I got no room for any more plans, any more anything."

For a moment they stared at one another in mute contention, as if they'd known each other for years and this argument were no more than a prescribed ritual for the release of emotion. Her breath was shallow, but it wasn't all fear. There was something challenging and provocative in her face. For a second Harry thought maybe Hazard was right, what she wanted was for him to be forceful; if only he had the courage to embrace her she would go soft in his arms. The ash fell from her cigarette.

"Go," she whispered. "Please go."

"Okay," he said. "Good luck with the audition."

She nodded.

"I really like you a lot," he said. He moved to the truck with loping smooth grace, swung the tools inside, then ducked inside himself. He waved, then the intensely red van spurted out of the courtyard. She didn't wave back until he was out of sight.

Harry sat numbly at the back of the bus headed for home, aware of the pistons pushing the lumbering vehicle down the boulevard for the sake of only one other rider besides himself. He felt gritty inside, full of another week dead and nothing done but another paycheck earned. There rose in him vague musings having to do with an equally vague plan. He tried to remember exactly when the idea had first occurred, but could not. He had even gone so far as to buy several sets of handcuffs and a disguise—but after all he wasn't a criminal, it was only idle dreaming, an obsessive touchstone of false hope.

The bus roared away leaving him in a cloud of diesel exhaust. He took out his harmonica and played a few bars as he climbed the long flight of steps that quartered a steep eroded bluff rising above the boulevard. He stooped and picked up a cigarette filter. On step sixty-eight he picked up a candy-bar wrapper and nearing the top several more cigarette ends and a beer can.

"Slobs," he said under his breath, then yelled: "Why don't you pick up this shit? Goddamn slobs!"

He stomped up the remaining stairs and entered the lobby of an oblong building of pink stucco that declaimed in peeling gilt letters: CASA DÉSIRÉE. He squinted at the slit in the mailbox, swore, then took the stairs three at a leap. He headed toward 307, the last apartment at the end of the hall, imagining his fellow residents as he passed their doors, feeling an obscure sympathy for each, though in two years of living there he'd barely exchanged more than common courtesies with any of them except old man Potter in 305.

Harry was jiggling the key in the second of three locks when Kirkwood Potter stepped out in an antiquated pin-striped suit, wearing a gray rumpled Stetson perched rakishly on his head. Potter had at one time ridden in rodeos and performed stunts in movies, and had even played small parts, "holding the horses," as he put it. Still fussing with the lock, Harry began to whistle, hoping his air of preoccupation would discourage the old man from launching into one of his reiterative tales of the wild west of Hollywood.

"Harry, my boy, just the man I wanted to see."

"Oh hi, Mr. Potter," Harry said, in a weak mimic of surprise which he was certain the old man recognized as phony.

"That dern lock givin' yeh trouble again? Heck, I'll loan yeh my gun and you can shoot the dern thing off," he said, then let out a tired guffaw that smelled richly of bourbon. Harry gave a quick grim smirk, trying not to look the old man in the face.

"I hope you didn't misplace your teeth again, Mr. Potter."

"My dern gums're sure sore, Harry."

"That's no excuse."

Behind Harry's door the phone began to ring. He panicked, struggling with the locks, thinking it was her. He burst through the door and picked up. The voice attacked before he had even brought the receiver to his ear: "Harry! Stevie Schlomo here. I been calling all day, man. I need the rest of the down payment. You told me today!"

Harry manufactured an absurd series of excuses while Potter tottered around the room, annoying him by freely handling his personal possessions, while throwing out obscene gestures which he indicated Harry should pass on verbally to the party on the telephone. Finally Harry persuaded Stevie to hold the car until the following day, promising to have the remaining $150 in cash. As soon as he had hung up, the old man grabbed his arm and shoved a stained manila envelope into his hand: "Take a look at them crackers, will yeh?"

The letterhead was familiar, the letter itself a short catalog of justifications for a monthly increase in rent. Harry shook his head: "It could be worse."

"Worse!" the old man sputtered. "Where'm I goin' to get an extra twenty bucks a month?"

"Take it easy, we'll figure something."

"We gotta discuss this, Harry. Yeh gotta help me."

"I just got off work, Mr. Potter, I'm beat."

"I know how yeh feel, Harry. Come over and unwind. I'll go fix the drinks. It's good bourbon, Harry. None of that cheap stuff."

"Thanks, Mr. Potter, but—"

"I'll be waitin' fer yeh," he said, and with a vehement shuffle he crossed the hall leaving Harry's door open behind him.

Harry got up and closed the door, cursing softly, trying to forget the old man, though he knew if he didn't show, Potter would come knocking. As soon as he'd turned over the third lock, a peculiar thought ran through his mind: *You're going to see me on TV soon.* The thought was so nonsensical it startled him. To distract himself he crossed the room and woke his pale blue parakeet, taking it from its cage on his finger. The bird hopped up his arm and fluttered onto his shoulder.

"You think I'm crazy, buddy boy?"

The bird twittered, and Harry whistled back. While he played with the bird he thought of the dancer, feeling sorry he had frightened her, wondering if he would dare approach her again. He had an impulse to call, and rehearsed how he would ask the motel switchboard for Miss Kruse, how she would pick up and tell him she'd been hoping he would call. Then what? *Hey honey, care to go out for a drink? Or maybe sashay over to my elegant abode, I'll show you my parakeet. Believe it or not he just flew in the window one day and started squawking at me like he'd known me all his life.* . . .

He returned the parakeet to its cage and moved to the window. The boulevard below was choked with traffic bound for a Saturday night ball game. The streetlamps suddenly illumined, evoking a nostalgia for time irrevocably lost; the sight both thrilled and terrified, as it always did, and he stood transfixed. *Lights*

> *I want to make something beautiful with lights*
> *a roadside tavern with lights all around*
>> *snow coming down and trees*
>> *colored lights on a pond      the snow*
>> *scraped away to skate      clean cold biting*
>> *my face      did I dream?      no*
>> *no      on the river in the calm widening      swirl*
>> *Mr. Hansen strung lights      over the river*
> *and built a fire and round and round in the big darkness*
>> *of winter night      with the bright lights*
>>> *we skated around the fire* . . .

He turned away from the window to the growing darkness of the room. The face of the alarm clock glowed. The receiver lay on the floor, quietly bleating. He looked at the bird asleep on his perch, head tucked under a wing. He looked so peaceful, so completely expressive and beautiful. For a moment Harry wondered why he couldn't have been born such a creature. Then Potter's insistent knock rattled his door.

Mr. Potter didn't even have a TV. He'd had to sell it the previous month to get up his rent. Harry had placed the ad and helped negotiate the sale. Afterward he'd promised to pick up a cheap set for him from the warehouse.

"Sit down, Harry, sit down."

Harry sat and stared at the rug. He could still see the pale square where the television set had been, the centerpiece of the room, the heartbeat of the old man's life, occasionally coughing up an old western in which Potter would appear for a few fleeting moments.

"Gotcherself a girl, Harry?"

Harry shook his head. "Not really."

"Gotta have a release, my boy. Not good fer the constitution if yeh don't. Kinder lubricates the whole system—" He coughed, caught his breath, then launched into a spasm of choking and gagging, during which he slopped some bourbon into a dirty tumbler and handed it to Harry.

"Yep, they usta go fer me. But that's not what we got together to discuss, is it? Now how're we goin' to get that dern Jew?"

"Well," Harry said tentatively, "he isn't a Jew, you know."

"I don't care what he is. How're we goin' to get 'im?"

"I guess if we had about fifty grand for a down payment, we could just buy this place like we were—"

"Fifty grand!" the old man echoed. "Whatcheh talkin' about?"

"That's how much we need, is all."

The old man tipped his bottle and appeared to ruminate on the vastness of the sum. He swore several times as he paced back and forth, gradually building into a familiar tirade about stars who'd cheated him, the government, the landlord, whatever ghost came to mind. In the midst of this litany, the old man snapped a pistol from his suitcoat and aimed it straight at Harry, eyes wide, face seething. Harry threw himself to the floor while Potter continued to rant, his eyes fixed and furious, the pistol quaking at the end of his arm.

"Harry? Where in tarnation are yeh?"

The old man's arm dropped and the momentum of the falling pistol threatened his balance.

"What in heck yeh doin' down there?" he asked, all violence gone from his voice.

"Hey, could I take a look at that gun, Mr. Potter?"

"Sure, Harry. Sure."

It was a heavy old polished revolver that looked more like a collector's item than a real weapon.

"Yep, gotta have a gun these days. We're livin' in a combat zone, my boy. Speakin' of which, y'll have to excuse me. Terrible thing when it's a major maneuver just to take a piddly leak."

While Potter was fuming behind the half-closed bathroom door, Harry hefted the gun, testing its weight. His finger eased onto the trigger. He tried to ignore the power transmitted by the feel of the weapon, but the thrill was undeniable.

When the old man returned, he hardly seemed to notice Harry was there. He slumped into his ragged overstuffed chair, muttering unintelligibly, staring at the spot once occupied by his television set. Then his head drooped and the big Stetson rolled off and he began to snore.

Harry placed the hat in the old man's lap and carefully pulled the door shut until the lock clicked. It wasn't until he was at his own door and his hand moved automatically for his keys that he discovered he had the gun. He didn't know why he had taken it, but he told himself it would not be in Potter's best interest to take it back.

He unlocked the door and stood inside, hovering indecisively, then stalked into the bathroom. He shaved rapidly, his face in constant animation, his shaky hand leaving a welter of nicks. He staunched the cuts with alum. The white powder dried in dark scabs that flaked off and the bleeding began again. Now he saw his face as he'd never seen it before: alive with a wrath he had thought himself incapable of.

He put on a jacket and tie and slipped the pistol awkwardly into his belt. The barrel jabbed coldly at his thigh.

His feet beat down the concrete steps, a frenzied rhythm that accelerated steadily, so he had all but lost control by the time he reached the bottom. He had no destination in mind, but let his feet lead him. For a while he walked, his gait steady, almost serene, past endless blocks of two- and three-story stucco apartments with absurdly romantic names embellishing their banal façades. He lost all sense of time and direction, as if he were moving in a state of free fall. Then he discovered he was running. Fog moved in, muffling the city with an eerie quiet that underscored the violence that gnawed at his body. Yet he was grateful for the fog; it allowed him to carry the old man's gun openly, occasionally aiming it at a headlamp, a streetlight, or the shadowy forms of shrubbery silhouetted against the buildings.

He came out of the residential district onto a commercial boulevard. A neon sign burned, bright pink letters: LIQUOR. He ran toward the sign; it seemed a mirage, like a shimmery stretch of desert road always moving ahead.

The fluorescent lights made him blink. The man had a round face, his head almost bald, his eyes pinched and snarling. The woman had peroxide curls and smoked a cigarette in a holder. They both stood still when he pointed the pistol at them and said: "This is a stickup."

They stood still for a long time. Harry waved the gun around.

The man said: "Listen, buddy, you drunk?"

"I need a hundred and fifty dollars."

The words felt heavy, ridiculous, unreal.

"A hundred and fifty," the man said. "You want me to write a check?"

Harry squeezed the trigger, aiming over them. His arm jerked. His ears rang. The air stank of gunpowder and alcohol. Pieces of glass kept falling from the shelf directly above where the man and the woman had been. Harry leapt onto the counter. They were squatting on the floor.

"Stand up," Harry said, still shocked that the pistol had gone off.

"Okay, buddy, just take it easy. Take it real easy."

"I'll pay you back," Harry said, and simultaneously was aware of activity behind him, someone entering and quickly exiting. "Hurry it up. I don't care anymore, you understand?"

"I understand, buddy. Just take it easy. I doubt we got a hundred and fifty."

The man opened the register and started counting money.

"Hurry up."

"Hey, guess what? We got it."

The man counted bills slowly onto the counter. Five, ten, twenty . . . The woman inched away.

"Don't move," Harry said.

"Harriet, just stay right here. This man just needs a loan. What's your name, buddy?"

"Hank," he said.

"Hank what?"

"Hank the bigshot!" he yelled and grabbed the money off the counter. Something hot bit his arm, throwing him off-balance. Glass was breaking at his feet. He glimpsed the woman, her arm jerking upward.

"Please don't," he said, backing up, Potter's pistol aimed right at her, his arm shaking. "Don't, lady, I beg you, don't."

Somebody pushed him and he heard another shot. The fog filled his lungs, condensed on the burning heat of his face. They were still shooting. When he glanced over his shoulder, the pink letters were a blur.

It didn't hurt, not nearly as much as he'd expected. He looked at his hand; the money was there. Out of sight, he slowed and started to whistle, trying not to worry about the bleeding. He whistled over the sirens and kept walking. He was whistling to beat the band, flying like a bird, a rare creature, rare and short-lived.

Blood had dried on the sheets. He woke, his head blasted with pain. The pain leapt, bounced around the room. A beam of light cut between the curtains. The parakeet began its noisome morning song.

"Hey, fella, it's your friend Harry. I look bad?" The bird chirped. Harry opened the cage and there was a flutter of pale blue around the room; then the bird perched on his shoulder.

"Yeah, old Harry pulled a job last night. Got shot. Look at that. Bitch almost got my eagle."

Indeed the bullet had passed through the flesh just above the tattoo on his left biceps, an eagle bearing a scroll with the motto: NEITHER MASTER NOR SLAVE.

While he was showering he got up the courage to look at the wound. The hole seemed too neat, a bit unreal. He dumped iodine into it, then danced around on one foot yowling. Yet he felt an odd pleasure: for the first time Harry experienced pain with a kind of satisfaction, and when the initial sting had died, he repeated the action. The crease on his temple, which he hadn't even noticed until then, didn't prove serious, but the bullet had burned a line in his hair over his right ear, which made him appear slightly lopsided.

"You coulda been dead, Harry," he mocked.

He dressed, went out to buy beer, returned, and drank. The pulsing in his head calmed. He played with the parakeet, gradually falling into an easy lassitude. When he lay down, he was instantly overcome by sleep.

He woke in a panic a few minutes before four o'clock, and remembered his deadline. His mouth tasted dark and foul, his head rang. He fumbled through his wallet and found a card. He dialed the number for Ace Used Cars, spent ten minutes begging Stevie Schlomo to wait, then ran to pick up the car.

Sunday dusk, the wheel under his fingertips, cruising the streets, his wallet empty, stomach empty, empty bottle clinking gently on the floor as he braked to a stop, radio up with that love song, that lovely love song, play it play it for Harry. A gaggle of young girls wave: he hits the horn that sings its five-toned song. They huddle, giggle, wave, blow kisses: O Harry, Harry, what you been waiting for, what you been waiting for all your life?

He downed the last beer, patted the pistol, and laughed, his laughter mingling with the love song pounding under the dash, the love song a lie but he didn't care, he loved it, loved everything, certain what he loved wouldn't hurt him, not even the dull heartbeat of pain in his arm, the crease in his temple.

He pulled the great car into the courtyard of the Rapier Motel, his foot gently touching the brake, the machine rocking in instant response. He swaggered out, pushed the heavy door closed.

Behind her door a television set babbled. For a moment doubt welled up through his intoxication. He turned to go, but the sight of the car buoyed him; she would want to come for a ride, surely she wasn't beyond that. And he couldn't forget the way their eyes had met, couldn't forget the change in her voice, or how she had opened the door under the pretext of needing the shampoo.

He knocked, the beat heavy, quick. Instantly he regretted the demanding tone and rhythm, and was relieved when

[ 37 ]

no one answered. He had just put the car in gear when her door opened. Her face appeared, bewildered, as if she'd been torn from sleep. She hunched inside her fur coat, clasping it close.

"Hey," he said with strained gaiety, "care to go for a spin?"

She stood staring with the same vacant gaze.

"Just picked it up an hour ago. Maiden voyage!"

Still she stood, peering as though at some alien creature who's just invited her to travel to outer space. Then, without any change in expression, she nodded, or he thought she did. The door closed sharply, the noise reverberating around the courtyard. He sat in confusion, hating his tameness. Then he leaped out of the car and pushed against her door. It was locked. He knocked again and again. The wound in his arm throbbed, and a trickle of blood slipped down his sleeve onto his closed fist.

She lay in bed with only her coat on, praying that if she just ignored him, he'd go away. His voice came faint and tentative through the door, and she cringed, keeping her eyes fixed on the television screen, every nerve pitched, her entire body listening. He was undoubtedly insane. Starting the fight at the club, then thinking out of sheer gratitude . . .

She picked up the phone, thinking to call the manager and demand he call the police. Then through the canned laughter, she heard his car start and squeal onto the boulevard. She sighed theatrically, and lay back watching the familiar program, letting it drug her. As she watched she found herself gloating over her survival of another episode she could only classify as bizarre. But the feeling quickly withered, and all she found to replace it was pure romantic fantasy: someday, when she was recognized as a great ballerina, and she had amazed the world with her endurance, her career lasting far into middle age, when it finally came time to enshrine the toeshoes and write her memoirs in some Mediterranean villa, she might mention this incident as typical of the hard days playing the barrooms, undiscovered except by the occasional crazy such as the TV man . . . her pen scratching on clean white paper, the balm of the Mediterranean through the window, tea brought by a bellhop in elegant uniform. . . . Kitty sighed. She'd held the manager off with halfhearted promises, and he had already leeringly suggested she might take care of her bill in a particular fashion.

"They're all alike," she said aloud. She thought of Lee Sandzone and cursed softly, knowing she would have to call him soon, perhaps allow herself to be rescued. The program ended and she switched through the channels, but she kept thinking of him: his arrival in the big car, his invitation, his actions at the club; and she knew she hadn't been fair, hadn't even felt about him the way she'd pretended.

She slipped off her coat and slid between the sheets, feeling their murky humidity from all the hours they'd held her body. Suddenly she wanted to weep. For hours, for days if necessary. But it disgusted her to know she would be weeping from self-pity, an emotion she had sworn she would cure herself of. So she swallowed her feelings and wallowed in the calculated romance of the late afternoon movie, wishing she had grown up in the fifties instead of a decade later with its tumult of protest and promise which she felt had been completely betrayed, leaving nothing but an impotent cynicism. At least in the fifties there had seemed to be something to hold on to; as insipid as those times had been, people did seem happy. While she watched and wished, without being conscious of it, she began to touch herself. She had no fantasy, simply a local sensation, and perhaps because she had no fantasy she didn't censor herself, letting half her mind cling to the fragile sensation, while the other half was immersed in the wash of images from the television screen. Now she began to grow wet, and she dipped her finger to pull the wetness out. This wetness itself pleased her almost as much as the sensation her finger made moving in its delicate circles, and for a moment she understood why a man could be so crazed for it, this slippery wet opening. Pandora's box, she thought. A silly slit that makes you vulnerable, everybody always wanting to stick things in. . . .

Despite this flare of bitterness, she began again to move, and now she turned over onto her hand and her hips rolled slowly in a mimicry of love. She wanted to find that urge, the same urge a man must feel: to fornicate, to conquer, to plant himself insistently in the woman, forcing her feeling out in the open so he could devour it.

A sharp rap on the door made her whirl. His voice came faintly through the door: "Hi, it's me, Harry."

"Go away."

"I can't," he said.

"Please, I don't want to see anyone."

"I'll wait until you do," he said.

She sat a long time, the arm she rested on trembling, her heart rushing as if impelled by some drug. Then she heard a harmonica. She got up and went to the door.

"All right," she said. "I'll be out in a minute."

She sat in the far corner bundled in her fur coat, the wind whipping the ashes off her cigarette, making it constantly glow. She looked straight ahead with a vacant gaze, like a prisoner being transported to a place of permanent incarceration. Every so often she would steal a glance and he would feel her eyes touch his face.

He drove with every attempt at appearing casual, conscious of his elbow sticking out and the sporadic throb of his wound, conscious of his two fingers on the wheel, of his body slumped slightly against the door. Cruising. The city transformed. It was always better at night, but this night it was magical with warm fog shaving the hard edges, and the hodgepodge of buildings endowed with a kind of cohesion by the scattered luminescence.

"Where are we going?" Her voice was calm, uninterested. They'd been driving for twenty minutes and he hadn't so much as offered to stop for a drink or something to eat: in a way she welcomed this break in tradition, yet part of her worried.

"I have a bird," he said. "Just flew in the window one day."

"That's nice," she said without irony.

"Like to see him?"

"Why not?" She sounded resigned, as if she'd just agreed to sleep with him. They were moving west on the section of Sunset Boulevard occupied by famous nightclubs, by offices disguised as Greek or Roman temples, the citadels of producers, agents, plastic surgeons. Huge billboards embellished with neon lettering loomed out of the fog with faces of superstars. It gave Harry a grand feeling to be riding down this boulevard with this girl wrapped in her fur coat, her eyes large, her mouth sensual and knowing, looking like a star herself.

They left the glittery section of the boulevard and entered an area of manicured lawns and floodlit façades. The fog opened and they traveled in the clear, then abruptly it closed around them again, the damp prickling their faces. He drove quickly, delighting in the immense car's ability to hold the curves as they descended toward the coast.

"Mind if I get stoned?" she said.

He pushed in the lighter, started to speak, and a smile broke on his face.

"You happy or something?" she said.

"Something like that."

"You're a strange one," she said with no particular emphasis.

"I don't know if I'm strange, but you are sure beautiful," he blurted.

"Huh," she said softly, but on her face a smile flickered. She inhaled, then passed the cigarette; he hesitated, not wanting to fall under the spell of the smoke, not wanting that thread of doubt hanging over anything they might say, afraid too the impulse to touch her might overwhelm him.

"What's the matter?" she said.

"It's just—"

"Just what?"

He shrugged, took the smoke, and felt the quick race of his heart, the warm flush on his face. He was so quick and needed so little. Not just with drugs. With so many things.

"Just what?" she repeated.

"It's just every time we've been together—"

"Yes, funny, isn't it?"

He shrugged. He didn't like the conversation: it seemed trivial and remote, yet at the same time invested with too great an intensity. And already his intoxication was leading to that magnification of sensation combined with sudden forgetfulness that made for wispy circles of emotion, like the incandescence of sparklers drawing letters against the darkness.

"Good question," he said and laughed, and the laughter caught in his head: in a flash he felt the joke of his life, of every action he'd regarded as momentous, even earth-shattering. There was no point in being serious. It was all a joke.

"Told you it was good stuff," she said.

He nodded, laughing, then took out his harmonica and played one-handed, his breath warming the instrument, his fingers reading the vibrations.

"Nice," she said when he'd finished, but for him her response seemed curiously subdued. He wanted to rouse her, wanted her to share his ebullient feelings.

When they reached the coast, the fog lifted, leaving the great expanse of sea glittering under a full moon. He pulled past a shuttered kiosk into a huge parking lot that stretched to the edge of the sand. The ocean breeze was warm and heavy, laden with the tropics.

"This where you live?"

He laughed. "I could put the roof up."

"Up or down, suit yourself," she said seriously. He watched her gaze drift over the expanse of breakers crashing luminescent and slow, then around to a neighboring car where two silhouettes swayed in embrace. He reached for her hand, then drew back as she turned to face him.

"Nice night," she said and there was a change in her tone, a kind of vitality, as if she'd suddenly woken. He felt his body lean toward her, yearning. She didn't shrink, simply sat watching, bemused. He touched her lips, but they remained inert, cold. To cover his embarrassment, he played a run on his harmonica and was thrilled when she opened her door and with a flurry danced barefooted across the sand, the fur coat swelling around her. He followed, still playing. When she reached the water she stopped and froze, her arms stretched toward the moon. He came up behind her. A wave broke at her feet, and she shrieked, kicking back into dry sand.

"They won't hurt," he said.

"What is it?"

"Grunion. They come up in the sand to spawn," he said.

With the next wave he caught one of the tiny fish in his hand and brought it to her, its slippery aliveness twisting madly. She gestured it away.

"Perfect for breakfast," he said.

"No thanks."

Each wave brought a fresh school that went flip-flopping over the wet sand, their bodies catching moonlight. It made him want to yell, all that incredible pulsing. Along with all the discarded beer cans and plastic utensils came millions of fish, silvery, clean, alive.

She was dancing just out of reach of the waves. She stripped off the heavy fur coat and he caught it, carried it while she danced, a marvelous nymph, totally different from the creature he'd witnessed at the motel.

"Look at the moon," she said, just to say something.

"Nice," he said.

"You think it's the same since they started tramping around on it?"

"Yes," he said.

"You know what I'd like to do? Dance up there, a real moondance."

"That would be great," he said. "You could probably jump a hundred feet. Just think . . ."

"Yes," she said, and there was, he thought, a hint of affection in her voice. She shivered and he held out her coat.

"Sometimes I just wish I could get on a plane, and . . ."

"Where would you go?"

"I don't know," she said. "Anywhere, I guess. Anywhere clean."

They walked, their hands close but not touching, weaving along the edge of the waves, wordless, engulfed in the spectacle of moon and water and fish.

As they approached the big white automobile marooned in the black asphalt lot, they began to speak, their conversation possessed by that strained quality that comes when words are provoked by some external force rather than inner desire: she was questioning his position and he saw no defense but to lie.

"So you fix TVs," she said, trying to keep her voice neutral. "Must be interesting."

He forced a laugh and took the opportunity to put his arm over her shoulder in what he hoped would seem a casual gesture. She stiffened, but tolerated this embrace, simply because it would have been equally clumsy to escape it.

"Not so interesting as a few other things I have in mind," he said.

"Care to go into them?"

"Don't think I know you well enough," he said recklessly.

She shrugged under his arm. A sick emptiness hit his stomach. He could feel her hurt, but he was helpless to fix it; he wished he could, just as he'd fixed the wing of the blue parakeet that he'd never thought to name.

"You're nice," she said suddenly, and pushed her head against his shoulder.

"Damn," he said softly.

"I still want to know about those ambitions," she said.

He looked into her face: it seemed utterly perfect, her eyes wide and clear, her mouth big soft open, and his mouth meeting hers, breath meeting kiss kiss oh christ . . .

"You're a tiger," she said laughing.

"Oh?" He grinned. Did I kiss you right? Been so long. . .

"Just don't get any ideas," she said.

"No."

"But you're nice. You're strange, but nice too."

"Thanks a million," he said.

"I know I'm supposed to hop right into bed with you, but . . ."

He flushed. God, he wanted to, oh jesus god but he was afraid.

"I have my period," she said.

"Okay," he said.

"You're not a bad guy. Listen, I'm not just a bar dancer."

"I know, I saw you were an artist. Really you are."

"I appreciate what you did."

They stopped.

"And you're so damn beautiful," he said.

"You think so?"

"Oh god yes."

Again their mouths came together. She let his hand fumble inside her pants, warm alive on her cool buttocks. He reached lower, finding the hot quick of her, and she thought: Oh shit, what if he knows I don't have it—and she pushed his hand away.

"My period."

"Okay," he said softly. "Okay."

She could hear the traffic on the boulevard below. The bird made fluttery noises in its cage. The lighted face of the alarm read 4:17. He was curled against her, his chest rising and falling against her back, one arm slung over her waist, his fingers grazing her navel. His penis rested small and warm in the crack of her buttocks, sleeping, without threat.

The posture of their lying together seemed to her more intimate than if they had made love. She felt a twinge of disappointment, but then she was glad he'd kept his word. She thought she wouldn't mind if he touched her now, but was afraid if she moved toward him, he might wake and misinterpret what she wanted. So she waited, trying to decide what she thought of him. She wanted it clear-cut: either to be in love or be aloof. But it wouldn't come clear. If she was going to love him, it should have happened already. It was Kitty's conviction that love was without choice, it was something fated, thrust on you; it was astrological, like birth and death. And since she wasn't in love with him, it seemed impossible she would ever be. Yet she wasn't indifferent—not as much as she wanted to be. There was something touching about him, something soft. For a moment she resented this softness: she hadn't asked for it, and it made her vulnerable.

She slipped away from him, and went to the bathroom, carefully shutting the door. When she came back she found his trousers at the bottom of the bed, and kneeling, watching him sleep, took out his wallet. There was no money, no credit cards. She opened a set of papers folded together, cracked and discolored: one was his birth certificate. He'd been born in Kansas. The other was his mother's death certificate dated five years after his birth to the day. A tiny worn and yellowed photograph fluttered to the floor. The woman was young, fragile, and something in her look seemed to say she was from another time. She returned the papers, found his driver's license and repeated his name. She was disappointed: it was so ordinary, without color or promise.

She wrapped herself in her coat; the silky lining cool against her skin evoked the startling image of how she'd undressed in front of him, even stripping off her underwear before slipping under the sheets.

She tiptoed into the kitchen. She was impressed with the room's cleanliness: no dirty dishes, no garbage, in fact the entire apartment seemed incredibly neat for a man living alone, though it distressed her to find almost no food.

She opened a door into a room she had not yet seen. Its one large window faced south, where a murky predawn light grayed the sky. The room was a garden: there were dozens of plants, about a quarter of them marijuana, luxuriant, full, standing three and four feet high. She wound her way between the plants, touching them, breathing in the hothouse luxury. She opened another door: a closet. From floor to ceiling were stacks of books, a mélange of titles, many of which she recognized as classics.

She returned to the kitchen, made coffee, and sat dazed from incomplete sleep, recalling their walk on the beach, the water surging around their feet, the tiny spawning fish wiggling against their ankles, the moon washing over them. Now at a safe distance, it appeared esthetic, pure, perfect, like a scene from a fabulous choreography.

His voice broke her reverie: "You made coffee."

He was dressed, still blowzy with sleep, his hair tousled.

"It's cold," she said.

"I was afraid you'd gone."

"I had to find out about your ambitions."

"Oh," he said numbly.

"And I've got a confession. I snooped in the bedroom. Quite a harvest."

He smiled. "Be ready in a month."

"So, what are you? a dealer?"

"In a way," he said simply, "except I deal people."

"You what?"

"I'm a people thief," he said, the lie liquid on his tongue. "Instead of jewels, it's people. That way I know where to fence them."

"Kidnapping," she said with theatrical hush.

"Listen, I'm kidding," he said.

She poked a cigarette into her mouth, her eyes never leaving his face: "How often you do this?"

"I was joking."

"I knew you weren't anyone run-of-the-mill," she said.

"My god, you're a real criminal." She reached and touched his hand. "But why the TV bit?" She stopped, then quickly answered herself, smoke pouring from her mouth: "Of course, it's a cover!"

"Let's forget this," he said.

"Harry." This was the first time she'd called him by name, and it was the first time his name had ever thrilled him. "Harry, how much do you get?"

"Forget it."

His body broke into sweat. Though he rarely smoked tobacco, he took her cigarette. His hand shook.

"You don't trust me, do you?"

"It's not that. . . ." Again he moved his mouth to the cigarette, trying to disguise his agitation.

"I'd be willing to help," she said. "It's like stealing dogs, then collecting the reward." In a whirl she was at the stove. "Harry, you need some coffee!"

He nodded.

"I bet your real name isn't Harry either." Then suddenly her movement was arrested by a thought: "Hey, you never did tell me what happened to your arm."

"Nothing. An accident at work."

"Yeah, I bet." She smirked.

"Believe what you want," he said, shrugging.

"Doesn't the FBI and police and everybody get all riled up?"

"It blows over," he said.

"Go on," she urged.

"There's nothing to tell."

"Harry, please. I trusted you. For all I know you're a psychopath. Anybody can come into a bar and offer a girl a fat tip and get on her good side."

"It's all a joke," he said. "I hate to say it, but it is."

"Ahh Harry, you can't fool me."

"I can't?" He shrugged in his peculiar way, looking a bit comical.

"No," she said, and spontaneously leaned across the table and kissed him, her tongue eager, assaulting. "I knew you were someone special. Now, tell me, Harry. Damn, this is fascinating! I knew you weren't exactly straight."

" 'Weird' is the way you put it," he said.

"You were being so mysterious. But don't think you'll get out of it this way. You've got to tell."

Once he started, he found it surprisingly simple, even pleasurable. She laughed and put her hand over his. "Harry, you're amazing."

He went on, warming to his own fabrication, "The strange thing is, most of them pay, not so much to get the person released as to avoid all the publicity. People get weird under pressure. Believe me, people with money are just as nutty as anybody, maybe worse. A lot of them are superstitious, and a lot of them have some skeletons in the closet they think are going to come out if they let the cops get in it. So they quietly take a fifty-grand loss. Maybe later, when they've thought about it a week or so, they timidly call the cops, who aren't all that excited since there's nobody to rescue. Now fifty grand from a bank, there's glory in getting that back, or a kid that's been snatched. But I never take a little kid."

"But jesus, what would happen if you got caught?"

The water on the stove boiled over and Kitty leapt to attend to it.

"If it gets that hot, you just let the person go. Forget the whole thing. Cops have their egos: it just isn't a heavy case when the patient is back home."

"The patient?"

He laughed softly. "The one you abduct. I always refer to them as my patients. The person buying them back is my client. I'm Doctor Cloud."

"Glad to meet you, Doctor." They shook hands and laughed.

"I've even had patients tell me they've enjoyed the expe-

[ 50 ]

rience. Most are teen-agers, and there's usually an underlying resentment of the parents."

"Amazing. Truly amazing."

"Not really. All very natural."

She gazed at him with perhaps desire, even a hint of awe.

"Harry . . ."

"Hi."

She blushed. "I'm just amazed."

"So now you could turn me in. They might be able to close a few files. If they could scrape up any hard evidence. Which I very much doubt."

"How many times have you—"

"Trade secret," he chuckled.

With sudden seriousness she said: "You don't really think I'd say anything."

"How do I know? The problem with this kind of work is you have to do it alone. Unless . . ."

She caught his eyes, and before he could turn away, she said, her voice a caress: "I like it. I really do."

They broke into wild laughter. It was all too easy. The very simplicity of it made it pure genius. Their laughter contained the confidence of this simplicity, the thrill of escape, the prospect of making dreams real: it was the laughter of children. Later Harry would remember this moment and its sealing stamp of conspiracy, and think perhaps it was the hysteria of lunatics. She was still laughing when his mouth met hers. Now, she thought, maybe I could do it now.

He took her hand, his face suddenly solemn, and led her to the unmade sofa bed. She followed with an anticipation both reluctant and eager, then sat on the edge of the bed with grim propriety. Their eyes met, and simultaneously, as if the movement were rehearsed, they fell back against the sheets.

For long minutes she bestowed on him all the over-elaborated kisses of an ardent schoolgirl. Without realizing it, they had stumbled onto the perfect game. For a while it was safe simply to kiss and want nothing more than to ride the carnival of sustained desire: it was a dream, delicate, evanescent.

Gradually the ache in his body swelled. His heart beat in his fingertips, his belly was smoke. His hand fumbled under her coat, went drunkenly into the heat, felt the electric damp; and with this touch he let escape a breath of longing so profound her skin seemed to recoil. How helpless he was, his eyes gone soft and swimmy. My god, she thought, he loves me. I could do anything, jesus those eyes, he's all shaky in love, poor bastard—

His face was against her belly, his hands locked on her hips, she silent, her body stiff, resistant. Her coat seemed to liquefy and disappear, leaving her bare to his assault. His mouth moved in her fur, his face obscenely rooted in her loins. She had to tell him, tell him she didn't want this. But when she tried to speak, there came only a harsh sighing he mistook for ecstasy, and his desire was so roused, he reached to loose himself. Now he moved up her body and kissed her mouth, but she remained slack, his breath beating against a lovely doll.

"What's wrong?"

"My period," she pleaded.

"I don't mind," he said.

"I can't," she said. "I wouldn't enjoy it."

Her words were a threat: for a second his face brooded over her with a violence that made her shrink.

"I don't get it," he said.

"I just went off the pill."

His anger deserted him in an instant. "It's okay, I've got something."

She was caught, the last logical objection shattered.

"Okay," she said. "But really, I'm not much in the mood."

He couldn't face her, couldn't reveal the shamed deflation this final utterance had brought. He got up, and in a turmoil of self-loathing, took refuge in the kitchen. He snatched the cup she had been drinking from, sneering at the smudge of lipstick her mouth had left, as if this were a symbol of all that was wrong with her. Without looking, he threw the cup out the window. A second later it smashed on the cement stairs that led to the boulevard. He stood there with the sound in his ears. The phone rang. It was like a knife going in.

When Harry picked up, Hazard announced himself in sharp cheery tones. There was no detectable change when Harry mumbled he was sick.

"Sorry to hear it, Harry. I just called to inform you your last check is waiting. Maybe you'd prefer I mail it out." Hazard stated this with absolute equanimity, a constant smile in his voice.

"I don't understand."

"Allow me to be blunt. We got a nineteen-inch color set missing out of your truck."

"You're kidding," Harry said. "Damn it, you got to be kidding!"

"Harry, I don't even want to know what you did with it—don't even care. Meany's is a high-efficiency operation and you're a bad component, my friend. It's that simple."

The line crackled. Harry tried to straighten his voice: "Just one more week. I'll get the set back. It was an emergency, I swear."

"Harry, one more week might be the week you go off the deep end. And I'm responsible, Harry. Believe me, this hurts me as much as it does you. Now just make it easy and let me mail the check out."

The fire in his belly rose; with repressed scorn he hissed: "Just make sure you deduct the cost of the stamp, okay?"

The response was a soft pattery laugh, then the connection broke. Harry spat into the dead receiver then slammed it down. He quickly folded the bed into the couch, furiously washed the dishes, all the while murmuring to himself as if alone. Then he let the bird out of its cage.

"Going to be out soon myself, fella. Out out out!" He laughed, and broke off abruptly when the bathroom door opened. She came forward with a light airy step, seeming utterly fresh, unconcerned. She kissed him lightly on the mouth: "I'm sorry," she said. "I really do have it. But it's almost over so—"

"It's okay," he said.

"You sure?"

"Sure," he said. "There's plenty of time, right?"

"Of course," she whispered. "You're somebody really special, you know?"

He wrapped his arms around her, and she burrowed into his embrace. It seemed eons since Saturday night when he'd taken the pistol and broken the chain of indecisiveness. His arm throbbed and the pain was a comfort: as a priest carries his rosary, the outlaw carries his wounds. Yes, he was Harry Keller, Outlaw. And he'd been an outlaw all along; it was simply a question of some spark. Suddenly he was overwhelmed by the marvel of his own aliveness. All the wasted days now flared with meaning: they'd all been necessary to get him to this one point. So it wasn't random! The pattern was there, like the pattern on an unfocused screen. You could be so close and never see it, then suddenly it could all come into focus. Even now, the curve of her back, the scent of her hair, all the events of her life and his wrapped together to make this moment. Until now he'd been seeing merely abstract dabs, but by some accident, he'd stepped back and seen the whole!

"You're shaking," she said.

"It's nothing. It's just I got to do something."

"Oh," she murmured, nestling. "Would you mind if I got my things?"

"No," he said distractedly. "No, that'd be great. There's an extra set of keys in the kitchen drawer."

"I know," she said. "Snoopy, aren't I?"

"It's okay."

She looked into his face with a steadiness he took as wonderment. She seemed to read his thoughts.

"I'll be all right," he said.

"You sure?"

He nodded and kissed her chastely on the cheek.

At a drivethrough liquor store he pushed his last change over the counter for two quarts of beer. He drove on, drinking rapidly, losing himself in a hit song on the radio. He was driving in circles, working on the second bottle, when he realized he was at the warehouse. He parked several blocks away, uncertain why he'd resolved not to display the car to his fellow workers. When he entered the work area, his gait was unsteady, and to his surprise he felt the old man's pistol in his hand. He stopped and attempted to hide the gun, half laughing at the vision of himself, shirt open, sweating, beery-breathed, twirling a Colt pistol.

The smooth cheery voice welcomed him over the intercom. He gave a low sweeping bow and marched toward Hazard's office, nodding to his astonished fellow workers. He climbed the stairs with deliberation. When he walked in, Hazard swung around in his chair and, without noticing the pistol, slapped Harry's shoulder: "Hope there's no hard feelings."

Harry snickered with showy exaggeration.

"Hell no, Mr. Hazard. Hell, you're just doing your job."

He brandished the pistol, feeling like a cowboy, then was struck by a ridiculous vision of himself as a young Potter hamming for the cameras.

"Harry, listen, I think you're a little—"

"A little what?"

"Listen, Harry," Hazard said, "I meant to tell you I'm

going to speak to Mr. Meany about the possibility of severance pay."

"You crumb. You sleazy little crumb."

"Harry, I know you feel bad about this, but let's be reasonable—"

Harry forced a burst of mocking laughter. Hazard seemed to cower, but the smile was still on his face. Below, the workmen had broken into haphazard milling. Men began to climb on the tables for a better view of the office. Someone cheered: "Go get 'em, Harry!"

Harry acknowledged the cheer with a wave and tentative smile, his threatening posture momentarily lapsing. Hazard quickly signed the yellow payroll check and handed it to Harry.

"No thanks," he said.

"What do you mean, Harry? It's yours."

"It's not enough. I want my severance pay. Now."

Hazard smiled: "Harry, you know I can't do that."

He patted the pistol and grinned. The perfect madman. The smile left Hazard's face and there were even sweat beads on the handsome brow. Harry trembled, terrified Hazard would call his bluff.

"Take it easy, Harry. Don't do something you might regret."

"Oh I wouldn't think of it," Harry said and scratched his chin with the pistol.

"Keller, I'm going to have to ask you to leave."

Harry remained in the same stance, still scratching his chin. Then he snapped his fingers, in caricature of a man alighting on a brilliant idea, the gesture itself seeming to regenerate his confidence: "I got it. Since this was all so sudden, and you didn't have time to arrange a going-away party, why don't we give the crew the rest of the week off? Paid in full."

Hazard regained his smile. "Harry, you're nuts, absolutely nuts."

Harry jabbed Hazard's belly with the gun. "So if I'm

nuts, maybe I don't care about a little squeeze, huh? Go on, turn on the mike, tell them they're getting a little free paid vacation in honor of Keller's untimely departure."

Hazard didn't move. Harry nudged him again with the gun. Hazard slowly picked up the microphone.

"Go on!" Harry said. "I got a lot of bad days in this gun." His heart raced. He had no idea if the gun was still loaded, or whether he even wanted it to be.

The intercom popped on. Downstairs in the workroom the men waited, hiding their tension with loose bantering. When the foreman made the announcement, there was silence. Then a smattering of applause. The workcrew then stood looking up at the office. No one moved. Harry emerged on the staircase: "Go on, you saps, the show's over. Move your asses out of this hellhole."

He fired several shots toward the ceiling. Fluorescent tubes shattered, raining glass on the confusion. He ran down the stairs and rampaged between the benches, knocking off gutted television sets. There were a few random cheers, but most of his co-workers simply scattered. Harry raced onto the loading dock, gave a triumphal whoop, then hopped into Mobile Unit 4 and tore off.

The van traveled west on Sunset Boulevard, then veered south and meandered down shady side streets that wound through fenced and guarded mansions, and without hesitation passed through open wrought-iron gates and moved rapidly up a long sloping drive. Harry found himself in front of a mansion in the colonial style of the South, with a long columned portico and tall French windows, a house that seemed like a movie set, something empty and exhausted, though there was no hint of outward decay. He half expected a butler in tails to appear on the steps, but nobody acknowledged his arrival.

Without awareness of movement or lapse in time, he was at the front door, raptly listening to the chimes echoing from within. Nobody answered. He rang again. A hot breeze rustled the eucalyptus. Sweat trickled under his arms. The immense brass latch was cool. Half praying it would be locked and his mission aborted, he pressed. A sharp clack and the door floated inward with liquid ease.

Inside the house the atmosphere was dark, the air thick, the quiet stifling. Though he had been without conscious intent, he realized now where he was. His gaze traveled over the familiar furniture, the paintings, a mantel holding an antique clock with golden angels trumpeting on the pendulum. His eyes began to seize on these alien objects, calculating their values, not in monetary terms but in the amount of drudgery possessing them would allow him to escape: this clock was worth a month of life, that chair worth three. He continued these calculations as he mounted the stairs, still unsure of his purpose. Panic overtook him, and he stopped, turned to descend, shrugged—then with frivolous abandon started back up. He remembered the den where he'd repaired the set, remembered the woman, tall, languorous, and striking, but something gone dead in her face. She'd left him alone, disappeared completely. And he'd almost regretted it, for despite her coldness, he had felt a peculiar attraction, had even fantasized a sexual encounter during which she lavished him with extravagant praise.

The den was empty. He went on down the hall to another room, its door ajar. He peered in. His breath stopped and he pressed against the wall. The gun shook in his hand. He made up impossible excuses for why he was there—but no one came to demand them.

The woman was asleep, sprawled back on the bed in a silk robe. Light filtered through curtains of subdued blue florals and caught the sweat on her forehead. Her breath was slow. She looked cold. Her skin was too shiny and clean.

He stood over her, his mind empty now of the momentary panic that had seized him when he first saw her, shocked that he could have entertained even the ridiculous fantasy he had. Just last Friday. He remembered her name: Fisk. This name one of thousands jumbled in his brain, owners of defective television sets whose habitats he'd briefly entered.

The woman had a note clasped in her right hand. He took it and read. The words had no more meaning than the name. They were simply words anyone might use, just as certain words are resorted to at funerals.

He read the words again, and felt a fleeting compunction for his fantasy, then a regret he hadn't acted on it. He touched her shoulder to see if she would wake. The woman didn't stir. He tucked the note back into her hand and took a pillow slip from the bed and began to fill it, scooping jewelry from the dressing table, adding antique brushes and combs. He rifled the drawers of her bureau and found nothing valuable. He moved quickly, but without haste or panic. Before leaving he took a fur coat from the closet and slung it over his shoulder, thinking Kitty would like it.

Intoxicated with manic boldness, he continued down the hall, suppressing an urge to whistle. Now it all seemed quite natural: the mistress of the house committing suicide, the front door unlocked, nobody answering the bell, no servants in sight; he felt invincible, as though part of him were outside looking on. He smiled at this vision, and as he did, doubt burst into his consciousness: the woman might wake, he might've left fingerprints and be implicated in her death.

A muffled thumping accompanied by a mournful wail broke his thoughts. The sound seemed to come from a great distance. He stopped, his body swaying slightly as if stirred by some unseen force. The noise was music, somewhat familiar, at times recognizably melodic.

He moved toward it, driven by a mirthful curiosity. At times the music seemed close, at times remote, as though its source were moving in an undeclared game of hide-and-seek. He entered a room, empty except for bed and bureau, its windows shuttered. The music felt close, vibrating the opposing door—then abruptly it ceased.

He reached the door and carefully set down the pillowcase. Something smelled acrid and sweet. He heard laughter, girlish, of indeterminate age. Then splashing followed by more laughter. The sloshing of water quieted. The girl hummed—then suddenly bellowed: "Fuck the world!" She laughed and repeated her proclamation. There was a harsh intake of breath and what sounded like sniffling. He inched open the door.

**66 I**'ll be damned if I'm going to feel guilty," she said,
rather enjoying the sound of her own voice, sensing its
moroseness would be touching if anyone happened to over-
hear. "I'll be damned," she repeated with exaggerated enun-
ciation. She cleared the steam from the mirrored tiles that
walled the tub and gazed at her reflection. She looked too
much like her father. There was an underlying sullenness she
didn't like. She tried grinning; it showed crooked teeth. She
stood up, continuing her examination. Her thighs were too
long and skinny, her hips too narrow, and no tits. Alice felt
about to weep: she wasn't sure why. Just out of boredom, or
having no place to go, or maybe it was her diminutive
breasts.

"You ought to run away," she suggested, then sighed
thinking of all the complications. "Stop thinking." She shook
a finger at herself. Then her mouth opened in startled surprise. In the mirror she saw her expression change while the
figure moved behind her. Then she saw herself sit down,
splashing into the water. And she distinctly heard him say:
"Please don't!" Then he sat down on the open commode.

Her whole body was jagged with uncontrollable laughter. She waved her arms trying to communicate to him that it
would pass, she meant no disrespect. Of course she should
have been terrified. It didn't make sense she wasn't; perhaps
he was too ridiculous, or not even real.

He got up and closed the cover, but he didn't sit. "I'm

[ 62 ]

not going to hurt you," he said. She still couldn't stop laughing. Fifteen, he thought. No, sixteen.

"Stand up," he said.

"I don't feel like it," she said.

"Okay," he said.

There was a long silence. They looked at one another. They both began to smile, then both bit down on their smiles, afraid. It was best to be serious.

"You're some sort of revolutionary, aren't you?" she suggested.

He shrugged.

"Don't be modest," she said. "Are you after the old man?"

"No," he said.

"He's a hypocrite, all right. But you're wasting your time. He's stubborn as a mule."

"I see," he said, and for the first time he realized the girl's nakedness and with the realization he felt compelled to turn away, as if his own awareness would trigger hers and with it alarm, perhaps hysteria.

"We don't really respect old men, do we?" she said sententiously. "You think we should?"

He didn't answer, still awed by her nakedness.

"Well?" she said peevishly. "Or are you above having opinions?"

"Depends on the old man," he said, but it seemed to make no difference to her that he'd answered. She gazed with a vacant wide-eyed stare.

"You'll have to come with me," he said.

"Did I scream?"

"Yes," he said.

"I'm pretty stoned."

"Aren't you a bit young?"

"You're funny," she said. "I could tell you weren't really going to use that gun." She was talking at an incredible pace, her words blurring in his mind. "What group you with?"

"I'm independent," he said.

[ 63 ]

"I like that."

"We'll have to go now."

"Whatcha after?"

"I said we'll have to go."

"Okay. I gotcha." She smiled coquettishly.

"You'll have to get dressed  Pack up a few things."

"Okay," she said.

She stood and wrapped herself in a towel. He followed her into her room and ordered her to dress, uneasily watching her lessening nakedness as a man might normally watch nakedness revealed. She dressed leisurely, with the meticulousness of one with a rendezvous. He nervously shook the pistol and told her to hurry it up.

"Don't worry," she said. "Nobody's around but Mother. And she's probably passed out."

"She is," he said.

"You saw her?"

He hesitated, calculating whether to tell.

"She's taken some pills," he said.

"Oh?"

"She left a note."

"That bitch," she said. "That goddamn bitch!"

"Take it easy."

"I'm just so sick of it!" she said. "I hope she makes it this time. But she won't. She knows just how many."

"I'm sorry," he said equivocally.

"Fuck you too," she said. "Let's get the fuck out of here."

She took a large, brightly painted plaster pig from her dresser and, casually raising it above her head, let it fall. Then she bent and hastily scooped handfuls of change and loose bills into a yellow canvas purse that seemed too unsophisticated and cheap. She ransacked drawers, throwing articles of clothing with erratic discrimination into a leather overnight bag. At the last second she tossed in a camera and a small locking diary.

"Come on," he said. "We don't have time for this."

She gave a mocking raise of her eyebrows and twirled model-like to display skintight blue jeans and a tangerine satin blouse knotted over her belly, but the display was heedless of him, an automatic assessment of her image in the full-length mirror. She froze, her eyes darting over the reflected image, then appearing to find the source of her dissatisfaction, she painted her mouth with crimson lip gloss.

"You're making me nervous," she said. "You aren't being cool."

At the door she turned and took a last look at the room. Then she broke from him, jumped onto her bed, and tore from the wall a color poster of a youth in black leather bearing a guitar. The girl spit, and shredded the image as she hissed and cursed.

"Enough!" he said.

She whirled. "Can't you see this is private!"

Harry reeled, stammering under her attack. "Okay, get it out of your system."

She kicked at the bunched and torn paper with deflated fury. "Okay," she said.

They stopped at the bedroom where the woman lay sprawled exactly as before. The girl looked at her, felt the pale, delicately veined wrist, pushed up an eyelid.

"You can make a call," he said.

"No thanks," she said softly. "This time she's on her own."

"I think you ought to."

"I said no thanks."

As they moved down the stairs, he found himself troubled by her cooperation, and became irritated with himself for being taken in. Despite her intoxication, despite whatever idiotic ideas she had about who he was, there should've been more resistance. In anger at the girl's equanimity and his own naïveté, he shoved the barrel against her spine.

"Jesus fucking A christ," she said, "Take it easy, willya?"

Using electrical cord, he lashed her hands behind her back, then made her lie in the van on a pile of padded quilts, where he bound her ankles. He tore off a corner of his shirt and tried to jam it into her mouth, but she spit it out.

"I told you I'd cooperate," she said.

When he tried again to force her mouth open, she caught his finger and bit down until he yowled. He slapped her and she started to cry. He lifted his arm to strike her again, then let it fall limp and simply cursed. Continuing to curse, he moved to the driver's seat, started the engine, and rammed it into gear. His limbs shook, invaded by the panic that had been held so long in check. He was driving too fast, and he knew it, but he felt that if he slowed, the fragile impetus that had driven him since the confrontation at the warehouse would run down, leaving him irretrievably scattered.

"Hey you! . . . Hey you, grasshopper," she said.

"Quiet," he hissed.

"You're scared," she said. "You'll blow it if you're scared."

He slapped the steering wheel. He wanted to pull over and make her shut her lousy mouth.

"You'd better shut it," he said, brandishing the pistol. He didn't like the sound of his voice.

"Take it easy," she said. "I told you I wasn't going to make trouble."

His heart hammering, his breath hard and tight, he felt the approaching rush of hyperventilation. He thought of the trumpeting angels on the mantelpiece clock and realized he'd left the pillowcase behind and lost the fur coat.

"Damn!"

"What's the matter, grasshopper?"

Without noticing, he'd driven to where he'd parked the car. The sight of the mammoth white convertible gave an immediate feeling of comfort, as if in a world suddenly devoid of loyalty, this machine had remained true.

"Hey grasshopper," the girl said. "I'm dying of thirst."

"Damn you, I told you to keep it shut," he said, feeling tears about to creep into his voice.

He executed a clumsy transfer of the bound girl from the van to the back seat of the car. As he took off into the gathering dusk, the mercury vapor lamps began to glow, reminding him of the moment at the window two days previous when he had experienced a kind of epiphany that had left him longing—even now his eyes began to sting, as if in mourning for the unrealized possibilities of his life.

"You're a mess," she said.

"Shut it up," he said, and without premeditation he turned and slapped her head with the gun. The sound caused his stomach to twist in a dry retch.

"You dirty shit," she cried. "You poor dirty shit."

"I'm sorry," he said.

"I bet you are."

"Please," he said.

He turned off the boulevard and set the car in low for the steep incline to the top of the hill. He parked and sat staring through the windshield, his face barren, as if awaiting a signal. Then with abrupt decisiveness he released her. She sat rubbing ankles and wrists. He wrapped the pistol in a brown bag, and motioned her out of the car.

"I had you all wrong," she said.

"No hard feelings."

"You're crazy. Really nuts."

[ 67 ]

"That's right, sister. So just walk and keep quiet."

"You know, all I'd have to do is scream."

"And all I have to do is squeeze."

"You're a bluff."

They walked in the deepening twilight, side by side, with clumsy jostling gait. A band of dark-haired children on tricycles broke around them yelling in Spanish; for a moment he expected them to stop and point accusingly at the paper sack rammed against the girl's ribs.

They passed a barrier at the dead end of the street, then skirted around the building to the back stairs, meeting no one. With the familiarity of territory, he began to feel more secure. He gave Alice the keys and made her open the door.

There was no one there. No note. The plastic clock lay on its side on the floor: 7:30. He could not believe so much time had elapsed.

"Kitty," he called out. There was no answer.

"Who's Kitty?" she demanded.

"Shut your trap."

"I need something to drink."

He took her to the kitchen and held the gun on her while she drank, gulping directly from the tap.

"Use a cup," he said.

She shook her head and kept drinking. He watched her bare midriff ripple, and thought: What a beautiful animal. As soon as she finished she went to the refrigerator and rifled through the odds and ends.

"Is this it?"

He realized how easily she rendered him powerless with her scorn. He picked up an apple and pushed it into her palm.

"It's mushy," she said.

Then he saw with instinctive insight what he must do— he had to use her method: to pretend this was nothing more than a lark. By assuming her attitude, he couldn't be controlled. He would even have to abandon the posture that she was his prisoner: she would have to assume that herself.

"You got any cigarettes?"

He found a half-empty pack and gave it to her. He watched her studied nonchalance in lighting the cigarette. She exhaled smoke through her nostrils: "What next?"

Their eyes met. Hers seemed utterly serene. She's playing games, he thought. Or she's so stoned she can't even see.

"When my partner gets back we can eat," he said.

"You know what I'd like?"

"I've got no idea."

"Jesus," she said. "You're so darn uptight."

He slammed the pistol against the table. She cringed, but more out of reflex than genuine fear.

"You're making me nervous with that darn fucking thing."

"Tough!"

"Please—" Instantly her eyes glassed over and she hovered on the edge of weeping. He stood over her, baffled, his throat too constricted to speak. Her head lolled, then fell against the table.

"Hey—you all right."

"Funny," she murmured.

"You feel dizzy or anything?"

"I feel like I've been here for years."

"That's not what I mean. I mean is your head okay?"

"I'm crashing is all—and I'm starved."

"Okay," he said. "I'll get you something."

"Avocados," she said. "And a nice dry chablis. Nothing too cheap, okay?"

"Sure," he said.

"You got enough money?"

"Don't worry about it. Listen, I didn't mean to hit you," he said.

"You're such a fucked-up spaz . . ." she whispered, and drifted off again.

He cleared a space in the plant room and made a pallet from a thin mattress and a pair of sleeping bags. He carried her dead weight to the room, marveling at the feel of her fragility. He laid her on the floor as one might set down a lifesized glass swan, his limbs shaking with excessive care. He brought out two pairs of store-bought handcuffs and snapped them onto her wrists and ankles. Tentatively he pushed a handkerchief into her mouth. She woke spitting, her eyes wide.

"What—what the fuck—"

"Nothing," he said.

She stared at him for what seemed forever, then her breath expelled in a long sigh.

"Just don't kill me, grasshopper. Don't get crazy and kill me." Then as quickly as she had waked, she was asleep again. He knelt beside her, watching. Then he bent and impulsively kissed her forehead.

When he had finished gagging her, he was overcome by an oppressive isolation, and simultaneously a ravenous hunger. He stuffed himself with stale leftovers which rested in his belly in a cold unassimilated ball. A dark thudding worried his breast. To distract himself from Kitty's absence, he paced fretfully, rehearsing his demands, thrashing for a precise sum. Fifty thousand. Seventy-five. One hundred. But these numbers were so immense as to be abstract; they opened a vertiginous space in his imagination. In desperation he arbitrarily fixed on the sum of seventy thousand. It has the right ring, he told himself.

The room grew dark. The darkness seemed to possess a febrile quality, as if night had been artificially invoked. Now for the first time he allowed himself to believe Kitty had abandoned him, but before he could speculate why, or rail against her, a key rattled in the door.

"Where were you?" he said with exaggerated calm.

"What?" Her voice dragged.

"I said where the hell—"

"I'm okay," she said, aimlessly waving a hand. She pushed past him, plunked down an overstuffed folding suitcase, and slumped onto the sofa: "I'm perfectly okay."

"I've got something to show you," he said.

"I'm beat," she mumbled. "I just need to rest, okay?"

He knelt beside her, but was afraid to touch her.

"Kitty, I got something important to tell you."

"Yeah? Go ahead."

"What'd you take?"

"A couple of lousy downers, if it's any of your business. It's been a bitch of a week, okay?"

He stood and walked to the window, all but hating her. Below him the boulevard was alive with traffic. It occurred to him for the first time that it was quite possible he was being pursued, not for the robbery or his spontaneous abduction, but for his mad display at the warehouse.

"I got to get out of here," he said.

"What?"

"I got the patient. Her name's Alice."

"Harry, what in god's name are you saying?"

"She's tied up. In the plant room."

"You what?" Kitty propped herself on one arm, her eyes

[ 71 ]

widening, the pupils huge. He came close. As the magnitude of what he had done began to dawn on him, he wanted her to hold him.

"Something bad happened," he said. "We got to get out of here."

She nodded, picking up his panic, but without any understanding.

"Come on," he said and dragged her to where Alice Fisk lay in a fetal curl, ankles and wrists handcuffed, mouth gagged. Her breath hissed faintly through her nostrils.

"My god," she said. "You really did it."

"That's right," he said.

A sickly grin worked on her face, then impulsively she embraced him: "I really didn't think—"

"I know," he said.

She hesitated a moment, then asked: "How much?"

"Seventy grand."

"But that's—you could get more."

"I know the limits," he said.

"I guess you do," she said. A spasm of contempt twisted her face. He turned away; he didn't want to insist, he wanted her to understand, to accept without undermining his fragile faith.

"We got to get out of here, then make the call," he said.

"I know," she said and offered a quick intense kiss which broke off as abruptly as it began. "Who is she?"

"Rich kid. And hates her daddy. She practically set up the whole thing herself."

"I just can't believe this," Kitty said.

"I know," he said. "What's so crazy is it's all so easy."

"Harry, I'm sorry about—"

"It's okay, really, it is."

The room was assaulted by a knock. They both froze. The knocking continued; Harry recognized it as Potter's, full of bourbon and loneliness. The old man began to crow in loud singsong about the sins of age.

"I'll get rid of him," Harry said.

The old man wheeled in, pushed by Harry, and bounded onto the couch.

"Up to a little hanky-pank, eh Harry?" He winked and slapped his thighs.

"Now Mr. Potter, we got to take off in a few minutes. Going to catch a movie."

The old man brightened: "I could go for a little entertainment myself. What picture is it?"

"It's sort of a private date, Mr. Potter."

The old man laughed in wet lascivious bursts: "One of them pornos, eh? Well, I couldn't afford no entertainment like that. Might break me." The old man cackled at his own joke. There was no response. A look of concern dulled Potter's face and his hands fluttered around his pockets. Finally he grinned, and held out a wad of small bills, his hand quaking.

"Here, take it."

"I don't understand," Harry said.

The old man looked hurt: "Why fer that TV. Fer that TV yeh was goin' to pick up for me."

"Mr. Potter, I haven't had a chance—" Harry urged the money back on the old man, but he stubbornly refused: "Hell, I'm too old to be impatient for anythin' but one thing." He broke into fresh guffaws that left him wheezing. When he finally caught his breath he said: "Yeh know, Harry, that dern pistol still ain't showed up. Wasn't I showin' it to yeh?"

"We really got to take off, Mr. Potter."

"What?" the old man said and appeared suddenly confused. Harry was caught: he felt Potter's aloneness as his own. "I said we have to"—and now he resented even having to raise his voice to communicate through the man's deafness— "we have to get going. Really." Harry led Potter across the hall, breaking what threatened to be an endless siege. Potter talked all the way, calling over his shoulder to Kitty to "make all the noise yeh want, honey." When Harry finally bid him goodnight, Potter grabbed his arm and leaned close. His words beat with rank breath: "Good luck, my boy." He winked and added in delighted conspiracy: "Harry, I got a nice little autermatic. I'd like yeh to have it, my boy. Jus' in case."

"I don't get it, Mr. Potter."

"I know yeh got itchy pants. Don't blame yeh. Now yeh sure yeh couldn't use that autermatic?"

"No, no I'm set." He felt miserable with guilt and almost broke down and confessed he'd snatched the pistol, but he feared the old man might want it back. And Harry felt a peculiar attachment to the gun; despite its being an impractical, cumbersome showgun, it was a talisman, the instrument that had impelled him into what he now regarded as his fate.

"Won't breathe a word," the old man said and savagely grabbed Harry's hand, the cool bony fingers clutching his with a passion that made him shudder. Harry felt suddenly weak, and tore himself away.

A few minutes past eight, Harry started to jockey the car out of its cramped parking space. His face was grim with anxiety, but underneath might be detected a sort of manic gaiety, as if the journey on which he was about to embark was the purpose for which he had been born. When the journey was over he would sleep—whether it would be the regenerating dreamless sleep of a man who had exhausted himself in an enterprise he had thought beyond his capability, or the sleep of death, he did not know.

He backed carefully, nudging the car behind. Then, without change in expression, he killed the engine and dumped the pistol in Kitty's lap.

"Harry, what—?"

"I'll be right back."

A protest rose in Kitty's throat, but she squelched it, as much on account of her own ragged exhaustion as her impulsive resolve to trust herself to what seemed to her, also, a destiny, though unlike Harry she saw an escape if the adventure were to go awry.

She watched blankly as he all but disappeared in a thickening fog, then caught a glimpse of him in the ill-lit lobby. From the back seat Alice stirred from drugged half-sleep: "Where'd he go?"

Kitty felt a flash of fear at this casual reminder the girl was ungagged, which seemed to her an act as rash as arming a prisoner. But the panic passed as quickly as it had come, leaving Kitty bewildered by her own change in attitude. Harry, at least for the moment, seemed right.

"I'm sorry it's been so crazy," Kitty said.

"I know it'd be against principles to trust me, but the point is . . ."

"What point?"

The girl didn't answer. Kitty turned and pulled the blanket over Alice's shoulders. Suddenly she felt alone. She lit a cigarette and turned on the radio; she caught the last half of a song, then the news broke in. She switched the radio off: it was as if all her terror, previously fixed on the local danger of the ungagged girl, had been transferred to the faceless abstract forces of institutional authority. Her fingers fidgeted nervously over her face. She finicked with a blemish on her right temple. Why doesn't the bastard hurry up? she thought. What was so god-awful important that he had to go back?

At that moment a car passed slowly and stopped at the battered dead-end barrier. Its lights died and both doors opened simultaneously. Two men stepped out of the car. Their hair was short and they wore open trenchcoats over subdued suits. As she watched them, she began to form the thought of who the men might be. A calm clarity lay under her fear; and she felt a disquieting relief that it was over and she could sleep. Perhaps some fame would come: she might be interviewed for magazines and television, perhaps receive an offer to appear in films.

The two men marched in authoritative symmetry through the break in the barrier, then proceeded along the heavily foliated walkway, two ghosts in the fog. She considered escape: it was conceivable only Harry would be apprehended. The car had not yet been transferred to Harry's name, so it would not be identified. The police would drive by and she would walk away. The girl would be found in a few hours. I could go back to Lee, she thought. At least for now.

[ 76 ]

Behind her Alice moved in restless sleep. The two shadows in the lobby moved toward the stairs. A third shadow appeared: Harry, holding the birdcage. He stopped and spoke to the men, his narrow frame hunched and friendly. Kitty could feel him smiling, could sense it by his posture. She did not move and she did not take her eyes from them. The gesticulations and postures of casual conversation continued. Maybe they're waiting, she thought. They'll follow, afraid if they take him now, the girl might be harmed.

Suddenly the two men were gone. She heard him whistling. The door opened and he set the cage behind the seat. He did not speak. When they turned the corner at the end of the block she let her breath go. "My god, didn't they know?"

He let loose a bubble of laughter. "I told them I knew him. I told them where he lived."

"Knew who?—My god, the idiots."

"I told them I heard him come in an hour ago. They didn't say who they were. But I knew you had to see them and I kept thinking she thinks it's all over. For a second I thought so too."

She giggled. "I did. I didn't know what to do."

"But we made it. It's a sign."

The car moved onto the freeway and as it picked up speed the convertible top billowed and began to hum. He handed her an open pint. The burn of whiskey mingled with the waves of thrilling terror running through her chest.

"Goddamn if I didn't walk right by the cops," he said.

They laughed. She couldn't recall when she had last felt so alive. She moved close to him. An omen! she thought. She didn't feel quite real. She needed to touch and be touched. She took his hand and led it between her legs; she kissed him, eagerly pushing against him. The car swerved. He broke away, and pulled back into his lane. She could not stop touching him. When her hands went to his waist, their laughter hushed.

His whole body seemed to quiver as she gently wrestled it out, already scalding and thick, leaping into her hand. Her hair fell over his lap and slowly her mouth took him in. A pang of fear came, then quickly passed in the heat of her reckless excitement. The wheels of the heavy car whirred and clicked on the harshly lit concrete. The fog broke and behind them spread a panorama of lights. Then the city began to disappear and the car moved past heavy trucks lumbering up the long grade into the mountains. By the time they reached the crest of the pass, the altitude had plugged her ears and she heard nothing but the minute sounds of her own breath. Then the car plunged toward the high desert and her ears loosened; she heard his voice thick with rapture. For a moment she wanted to pull away, to avoid the feel and taste. A long second passed when the whole world seemed in suspension. Still she held him. Then he broke and released. His breath came in sharp cries. Her mouth filled. She swallowed. A fire moved in her. Through the slant of the windshield she looked up from his lap into a blanket of stars.

Alice drew the rough wool blanket over her head and clutched it tightly to her body. Road vibrations tingled in her, the pulse of a journey she still didn't quite believe. At least it had broken the awful boredom. Suddenly she thought: I want to go home. She thought of them: of Mother Marion, of Daddy Nathaniel, and the thought brought a ripple of tenderness, then a petulant smirk. Let them sweat it.

The vibrations changed, and there was a change in the texture of the darkness. The radio went staticky, then twittered through different stations. The car had stopped. The door opened and she felt a gust of cold through the blanket. They were talking. The dumb bozos were talking. Maybe I should scream? The door slammed shut.

After a while the car door opened again and he was talking to her. She felt his hand on her shoulder.

"Come on, Alice, you got to talk to your father."

Let the bozo wait. . . .

"Alice, wake up."

Pitiful, really pitiful . . .

"He doesn't believe us."

"No skin off my teeth," she said.

"Now," he ordered.

"What if I don't?"

No answer. She smirked. She felt him grab the blanket. She held on, thinking she could feel the nervous sparks leap off his brain.

"Leave me alone!"

"All right, Alice, you give me no choice."

He gave a great yank and she let go. The blanket jerked off and she heard him fall. The woman was pointing the gun straight in her face.

"Damn it, Alice—"

"You got to promise not to hit me," she said.

His voice was a frantic whisper: "I won't unless you get out of line."

"And no handcuffs," she insisted.

"I can't do that."

"Then I'll go crazy. You'll have to kill me. They'll hound you to death, you dumb grasshopper. You think I'm scared just because you are."

"Everybody's afraid to die," he whispered. "Don't kid me."

"You think so? Try me. You won't even have to look. Just blast away, you dumb bozo."

She wasn't the least afraid; so it wasn't a bluff. This puzzled her. Maybe deep down I really don't care about anything, she thought.

She could see his hands shake when he undid the cuffs. But the woman was her real worry: her face was so white it gave Alice the chills.

"Would you tell her not to point that damn thing at me?" she said.

Harry took the gun.

"Come on," he said. "Just tell him everything's fine."

There was a phone booth about twenty yards from a stucco filling station, weathered plywood nailed over the windows. In front was a red hand-cranked pump with the glass reservoir still intact. Behind the station a paintless clapboard house tilted, as if it might fold at any second. The wind made it creak and groan. There was no streetlight, no traffic on the road.

"Where are we?"

"Hurry it up," he said.

All the panels of the booth had been kicked out. Dust and scraps of paper gusted in a cold whirlwind around her feet.

"I don't like it here," she said.

He picked up the dangling receiver and put it in her hand. She simply held it and said nothing. He prodded her with the gun. Her voice cracked: "Hello?"

"Allie?" His voice was strained and remote, the edges ragged with anger and shock. She tried not to, but she felt sorry for him. But I won't feel guilty, she told herself.

"Alice, if this is one of your shenanigans I hope you'll tell me immediately."

"I hope you're okay," she said.

"Alice, did you hear me?"

"Yes."

"I want you to know your mother's doing fine. There's no danger. Of course she was quite upset—"

"I know, Daddy, I know."

"Alice, did you have anything to do with this? Now I want the truth."

The line crackled with static, and she pulled the receiver from her ear. "You big dummy," she mumbled.

"What?"

"Of course not!"

"Now Alice, you listen carefully—you *are* all right, I trust. Nobody's doing anything—molesting or —"

"I'm fine, Daddy. Really." I hate you, she thought. *Molesting.* This guy couldn't molest a sheep.

"Are they terrorists, politicos, what?"

"Are you going to pay them?"

"Damn it, Alice, would you answer me?"

"I wish you'd just pay them so I can come home. I'm scared." But her voice wasn't convincing.

"Where are you, do you know that much?"

She covered the receiver and turned to Harry. "He wants to know where we are."

Harry snatched the phone: "Okay, Mr. Fisk, I think you got the picture."

The man cleared his throat. "Whoever you are, I urge you to give up this crackpot scheme."

"You just put the cash together, Mr. Fisk. Real quiet. The only news report I want to hear is no news."

"Who in hell do you think I am? I don't control the goddamn press."

"You just control yourself, Mr. Fisk, and nobody'll know, not the press, not the cops, nobody."

"Listen, Cloud, I'm afraid it's already too late on that account."

"You better make it not too late."

The operator broke in. "That will be an additional dollar and seventy-five cents for the next three minutes, sir."

"I'm done, operator," Harry said. "I'm done." He slammed down the receiver. "All right," he said. "Now get back in the car."

Alice didn't move. "You're going to blow it," she said, singsong. "You got to be cool." He did look cool. Shivering like a chicken. "I got to pee, grasshopper."

"Then pee, for christ's sake."

"And just where, might I ask?"

"Just squat down and pee like everyone else."

"Not in front of you, I don't."

Kitty yelled from the car: "What's going on? I'm freezing."

"Squat," Harry said.

"Forget it," Alice said.

"Squat, damn it!"

"I don't have to anymore."

"Don't make me get rough, Alice."

She turned and marched in deliberate undulations toward the car, then stopped. "You know, I just love brilliant rough young dudes like yourself," she said, and with a smirk she ducked inside.

The unmarked blacktop swallowed the headbeams so completely, at times he lost track of the road. The last clear radio station had been consumed by static for over an hour. For a second the lights caught a sign, a weathered arrow of wood pointing toward the sky, with peeling black letters: DEVIL'S PLAYGROUND. The two women slept. He was driving east toward a barrier of ragged bluffs outlined by a faint gray breath of false dawn. His head nodded. The road fell away and the car dropped, its springs banging in sharp contraction. The steering went watery and the car slowed, stones peppering the floorboards. He fought the wheel, leaning his weight in futile instinct against the inertia of the spin. I didn't see it, he thought, didn't see the road gone.

The dust moved and a cow ambled like some prehistoric figment across the beams. The voices of the women in sleepy complaint came to him without meaning, a vague muffled babbling mixed with the sharp squawking of the bird and a distant mournful lowing.

"It's all right," he said, as much to himself and the bird as the others. He started the engine and set the car in reverse; the car rocked and heaved, then the tires took grip and it catapulted back onto the road.

He drove slowly, eyes straining for the ill-defined shoulders. Occasionally cattle would be bunched in his path and they would stand lowing and blinking until the white hood nudged into them, forcing a separation, their bulky bodies bumping the fenders in lazy challenge, and in his half-sleep, he would ask himself: What are they doing wandering around like this? How did I get on this road? Finally he pulled over. His eyes fell shut and his chin hit his chest. Dust and sage and tumbleweed paraded through the beams as the three slept.

His blood seemed to have gone cold: every muscle was stiff, as if he had been sleeping for weeks, not hours. He sensed a warmth outside, prodding in. He pushed aside the jacket covering his head. Sun slapped his face. The parakeet fluttered in its cage and sang. The car was still idling, so he had only to put it in gear and start off. A bluff appeared, then disappeared in the rearview mirror. From the back seat, Alice complained of needing to relieve herself. After several such complaints, he pulled over and released her from the handcuffs. She skidded into a ditch and squatted, then as soon as Harry had turned his back she stood and began to walk, hips slim as a boy's in faded blue jeans, the pale towhead catching highlights of midmorning sun. She moved with slow steady strides as in a sleepwalker's trance, and in less than half a minute she disappeared into high desert chaparral.

Kitty looked, squinting against the sun. The girl's disappearance defied logic: Kitty was sure she'd never taken her eyes off her. But Alice was gone, absolutely gone, as if snatched by some supernatural force.

They didn't call for her, simply ran in frantic bursts from one clump of chaparral to the next. From the road the vegetation had not appeared as thick and tall as it was, nor had the desert seemed so vast. They moved aimlessly, their faces smudged with dirt, and when they blinked fine grit rubbed their eyes. Kitty coughed, body slack, panting. Fifty yards to the south, Harry yelled: "You shoulda watched her, you dumb bitch, you shoulda watched!"

Kitty started to yell back, then simply shrugged, spent beyond defense.

"This isn't a goddamn game," he screamed. He ran, his feet churning spasmodically in the arid soil. His legs began to sag. He kicked through a pile of bones. He could no longer see Kitty. He fired the pistol and demanded the girl appear. The reverberations echoed. He fired again. From far off came the sound of the horn, bleating its frivolous five tones with sarcastic gaiety.

When Harry reached the car, before Alice could speak, he hit her, cuffing her face with the back of his hand. The look in his eyes frightened her more than the blows: he was frantic, a man hunted, a man close to death. After the third blow, tears sprung to his eyes, and his energy began to falter. Kitty arrived, shrieking at him to stop. He turned, his arm raised to strike her—then he sprinted down the road. He did not stop running until he was a quarter-mile away. He stood absolutely still, like something petrified.

He wanted to give up, to lie down and rest; his mind needed a white wall. His shoulders began to shake. Dust swirled around him. He cursed himself for a weakling. Then suddenly he was empty; there was nothing to be sorry for. He turned and walked back to the car, and without a word of explanation, he handcuffed Alice and they took off.

He drove lackadaisically, with a defiant aimlessness, as if all danger had magically vanished. When he stopped for fuel, he bought beer despite their shortage of funds. Alice dug four worn one-dollar bills from her purse, and away from Kitty's gaze, offered them. After a moment of hesitation, he stuffed them into his pocket. An hour later he caught her glance in the mirror and tacitly thanked her.

They drove on, and while wind whipped through the open car, they abandoned themselves to beer and cigarettes and motion. His intoxication immersed him in the feel of the road, in the subtle vibrations of the wheel under his fingers. Periodically Alice brought out her camera, Harry unlocked her handcuffs, and they all piled out to take snapshots of themselves before a scenic view. Occasionally the radio picked up a station, and they would sing along, ebullient, entranced. For a second Harry saw the convertible as though it were suspended against a moving desert backdrop, with the three of them gaily singing, a trio on a summer lark.

At ten o'clock that night, the gay mood of the day was shattered by the first news report of Alice's abduction; it came in staticky broken segments, punctuated by an accelerating stream of curses from Harry. He beat against the steering wheel, and threatened Alice.

"You didn't tell me your old man was a goddamn senator, for christ's sake!"

Alice shrugged good-naturedly: "You never asked."

"But I thought that was why," Alice said solemnly. "You really didn't know?"

"Jesus christ, the big professional criminal," Kitty sneered.

"But I thought that was why," Alice said solemnly. "You really didn't know?"

"Why in hell should I?" he hissed.

"Oh christ," Kitty said. "I don't fuckin' believe this."

"Shut up," Harry yelled. "Both of you just keep your goddamn traps shut!"

An uneasy quiet settled over the car. Finally the two women dozed. Harry drove in a weary trance, trying not to let the full absurdity of his ignorance overwhelm him.

He passed a cinderblock tavern, then slowed for a forty-five-mile-limit sign and passed under the flashing light of a one-stoplight desert town somewhere east of the Sierra. He passed the dusty brick and clapboard façades and on the northern outskirts spotted a telephone booth. He dug out a handful of change and made the call. It rang a long time before there was any answer. By then his entire arm ached from clenching the receiver.

The man didn't sound like Fisk. His voice was cracked, blurry, out of control. The man had been drinking. It was a cop imitating Fisk. They were trying to trick him. A goddamn doublecross.

It took a minute before the man convinced him he was indeed Nathaniel Fisk. Harry demanded to know why the story had been released to the press. The senator explained in weary tones how Mrs. Fisk had regained consciousness and reported Alice missing, how when the tapes from the automatic surveillance equipment were reviewed someone let something slip to the press.

"I'm not buying that, Fisk. It sounds flimsy as hell."

The man cleared his throat, coughed, then seemed to lose his voice.

"Mr. Fisk?"

"You don't seem to understand. I'm in the public eye."

It was a fist in Harry's face: the whole damn country was going to be after him.

"Cloud? Are you there?"

"I imagine this is being recorded," Harry said.

There was a long fuzzy pause, then the senator's voice: "I'm getting the money. It'll be ready this Friday, just as you asked."

"Mr. Fisk, this is no goddamn joke. I want to know if you're recording this conversation."

"Please," the senator said. "I'll pay the money. I don't need it. I've tried to persuade them to let you and me handle it."

"I got to think," Harry said. A diesel roared past leaving its mournful wake of fumes. Wind rattled the open door of the booth.

"Cloud?"

"Your daughter's in trouble, Fisk. You high and mighty bastards assume we do this for fun—your daughter doesn't mean a damn thing to me." He was ranting. He wanted to stop, but he couldn't. Out of his own fear, he threatened disfigurement, death. Then he collapsed, hunched with the receiver against his chest, his back to the car, not wanting them to see. He could hear the faint metallic buzz of the senator's voice. Damn him, Harry said. Damn him, he's going

[ 89 ]

to make me do it. Going to make me do something bad.

"Cloud, I can't hear you—is she all right? I want to speak to her."

"You didn't keep your word, Mr. Fisk." Harry's voice was a whisper no louder than the wind.

"I can't convince you, Cloud. You'll only believe what you want. Just don't hurt her. For your own sake. I'll do everything I can. I won't press charges."

"There won't be any charges. They'll never find us, you see—"

"Cloud, please listen. You tell me what to do."

"I want that damn money. I want it now."

"I'm doing everything, believe me. It's just a question of practicality. Of not drawing attention—"

"God damn it! It was on the goddamn news, for christ's sake!"

"Yes. All right, Cloud. That doesn't mean I had anything to do with it. I'll have it Friday. Just tell me where—"

"You'll get a call. Thursday night. Nine o'clock."

"I'm a man of my word, Cloud."

"So am I, Mr. Fisk. If I get caught, believe me, there'll be revenge. I'm not alone. If they get me, someone else will be there to hunt you down. Someone will get you or your wife or daughter, you understand?"

"I understand. You get the money and you'll let her go. And I'll see to it you won't get caught."

The man was so convincing that before Harry realized what he was saying, he had thanked him. The senator cleared his throat: "Well, yes, I think we understand each other, Cloud. I just wish you didn't have to do it this way."

"What other way was there, senator—apply for a goddamn grant?"

"I told you, I understood. I'm sorry about—"

"You'll need a courier, Fisk, someone who can afford to be gone a day or two. Someone inconspicuous."

"But, how can I—"

"Come on, Fisk. You hire somebody. And get that damn recorder off the line."

"There is no recorder."

"That's crap, Fisk! That's goddamn crap! How am I supposed to trust you when you give me crap like that?"

"Listen, Cloud, they barged in on me. Now don't do anything rash. I'll see to it they take it off."

"Get rid of it, get rid of them. I don't care how." He broke the connection. His heart skipped, random and frenzied. Sweat turned cold on his neck. He stumbled behind the station to urinate; dribbles splashed on his hand, blown back by the wind.

At two o'clock that morning, the car began to skip and buck. Kitty stirred, murmured: "Where are we?"

"Wherever we are, we're almost out of gas," he said, his voice clinging to that even calm that comes with extreme alarm.

"You got to be kidding."

His answer was a broad sardonic smile. He cut the engine and let the car roll, periodically turning on the ignition to allow the engine to catch and sputter them into lurching momentum. They passed a sign: OASIS, POP. 93. The heavy automobile rolled slowly down the practically imperceptible incline of a dingy main street with three streetlamps, a general store, a closed filling station. They looked at each other: their faces wan, frantic, immobile. The car stopped.

"Welcome to Oasis," he said.

"Everything's a joke with you, isn't it?"

"Not everything," he said.

He got out and ran across the road to a two-story clapboard house almost devoid of paint, its peeling latticework overgrown with dusty ivy. At the side of the house he found a garden hose from which he cut a length, and an old galvanized sprinkler can. Kitty watched him reappear with the can and the hose coiled around his arm. Her jaws moved in grim rhythm over a stiffening wad of gum as she shivered in the cooling car.

Fifty yards past the house, Harry found a vehicle without a locked cap, inserted the hose and sucked the burning fumes, coughed, and sucked again. Kitty watched him coming, weaving as though drunk, the heavy can banging his leg. He knocked the sprinkler head off the can and poured the gasoline. He was spitting, his eyes tearing and burning. Alice's face pressed against the window. The door opened and Kitty got out.

"What's happening?"

He tried to move his mouth.

"Harry, are you all right?"

"Got a mouthful of gas."

"Jesus! How could you be so stupid!"

Dizzy, he sat down. She helped him up and while he leaned against the car, she poured the rest of the gasoline. It took a long time for the car to fire: when it caught there came a sleepy "hurrah" from the back seat.

Harry stopped beside the battered sedan from which he had siphoned the gasoline. He took out the four dollars Alice had given him and clipped it under the wiper blade.

"You're nuts," Kitty said. "You really want to blow it, don't you?"

"Look how old his car is."

"Harry, we're out of goddamn money!"

He stood looking up at the stars, and with pathetic melodrama lifted his arms as if in supplication.

"You're crazy. You're a loser, Harry. I should've seen it that first night."

He whirled, fist drawn, voice trembling: "Don't you say that. Don't you ever say that again!"

In the next town he siphoned two more cans of gasoline, stubbornly leaving a promissory note on each of the cars. They kept pushing on, their stomachs pitched on hunger, their minds testy with exhaustion. The terrain rose and fell in bleak monotony, its vastness eerie in the predawn light. Shadows leapt and crawled over the road. Harry began to hallucinate. At some point he realized the road was edging more north than east and they had crossed a state line, but a few minutes later he was unsure which state they were in. Finally his eyes refused to stay open and he pulled onto the shoulder.

Harry woke to the labored growl of a truck crawling the long incline, then fell back into uneasy sleep, only to wake again with a light prying his eyes. He started, sat up, his hands against the beam. There was a rapping on the window. He reached for the pistol, then some half-blind vision of a uniform stopped him.

They were speaking to him, the one with the light gesturing to roll the window down. Fleetingly he thought he should fight, make a last go of it.

The other one was smiling. His badge glinted. The uniforms were unfamiliar.

"Heck of a spot to camp out," the officer said. His cheer jarred in the desert cold.

"Yeah, we just—"

"Look a little lost." The flashlight played around the car, lighted on the birdcage.

"It's for my mother," Harry said.

"My wife used to raise them," the officer said.

"I'm taking it to my mother up in Reno."

"Kind of off the track for Reno, aren't ya?"

"I guess so."

Again the light moved around the interior of the car. Kitty stirred. Harry prayed Alice would stay asleep. He had the feeling the officer could talk a long time.

"I wouldn't recommend sleeping in an idling vehicle. Me and my partner found a pair about four o'clock one morning over by Beatty curled up nice and stiff. Not a mark on 'em."

"Thanks," Harry said. "I hadn't thought of it."

The officer outlined a route to Reno, recommending a

motel in a neighboring town. The cruiser pulled away. From
the back seat came a gleeful snort: "Hey grasshopper, I bet
you were about to piss your pants, huh?"

He started to speak, but whatever it was he was about to
say left him. He was shocked by what seemed to him a second miraculous escape. It made him feel insubstantial. Then
for a moment he allowed himself to be charmed by his own
innocence, and actually harbored the reckless idea that some
abstract force was protecting him.

"So don't you see, grasshopper? Don't you see all I had
to do was—"

"Yes, I see," he said.

"So you can trust me."

"How long?" he said. "Until you get sick of playing the
game?"

"Until you get the money," she said. "Isn't that fair?"

He started the car.

"What I'm trying to say, grasshopper, is I want these
damn things off. They're going to make me scream."

He had already forgotten what it was she had said. Then
she screamed. She wouldn't stop. Kitty woke and she too
began to yell. In league, they ordered him to do something.

The immense white automobile skidded to a stop. At
the far side of a valley, perhaps twenty miles distant, he
could see the outline of mountains against a paling sky. He
stared at the mountains for what seemed a long time, then
abruptly announced: "You can both get out. We'll forget the
whole damn thing."

"Don't be ridiculous," Kitty said.

"I want these damn things off," Alice said.

"All right," he said, but when he began to unlock them,
Kitty objected. Once more Alice started to scream.

"Do something," Kitty said.

Harry undid the handcuffs. Kitty sulked with a cigarette.
Alice wanted to sing. Nobody wanted to sing with her.

"Are you going to let her?" Kitty said.

"Be quiet," Harry said. "I can't think."

Alice let out a mocking snigger and pulled the blanket over her head.

An hour later they left the dreary desert terrain and entered the forests of the eastern Sierra. The trees themselves brought a primeval relief, an offer of refuge. So when Harry pulled off onto a dirt road, nobody questioned him. It was as if they were all in mute agreement that they had to stop, for the car and the open highway had become a kind of prison.

A hundred yards in, he was forced to stop and remove the poles from a wooden barricade. After that, the road gradually narrowed and the undergrowth thickened until the tracks were all but obliterated. Saplings bent under the front bumper, scraped along the undercarriage, and sprang up behind. Finally the road descended sharply to a clearing where a log cabin stood; behind it the glitter of water. The lake, which they would christen Paradise Pond, was spring-fed, two miles long and a half-mile wide. They sat for several minutes as if witnessing a dream rather than any palpable landscape.

Alice was the first to get out; in slow languorous motions she stretched her limbs. At that moment she appeared no more captive than the crow that swooped through the clearing, its cries breaking the forest hush. Alice called to the bird, and then, as if answering, a breeze stirred high and murmurous in the pines.

The back door was closed with a simple latch. They entered a kitchen with a sink and hand pump and a four-burner woodstove that was set on planks to distribute its weight across the floor. There were no provisions other than a tin of oatmeal and a jar of sugar. In the main room was a fieldstone hearth cleaned of ashes, with several split logs waiting on the andirons. Above this main room was a large sleeping loft accessible by a set of open stairs cut from halved logs. A door to the right of the fireplace led to a tiny room dominated by a swaybacked bed with a thin bare mattress.

Harry opened the front door and walked onto a veranda

that ran the length of the façade. As he stood looking at the mirror-smooth lake, Alice ran past him down to the water and out on the rickety dock that shook even under her slender weight. Then, by some display of sleight of hand, in a fraction of a second, her clothes were gone. The pale sliver of a body, with its high rump and almost breastless chest, lofted and flew parallel to the glitter of water, and then without seeming to disrupt the glassy surface, was under it, visible in watery distortion, moving like some creature more amphibian than human. She stayed under a long time, disappearing, then bobbed up with an expulsion of breath, her head swinging, spreading a lace of droplets across the unruffled surface. She waved to him. Before he waved back, he felt Kitty's gaze against his face, and knew that his expression, even through the wanness of fatigue, must betray his fascination. He turned away, his wave tentative and shamed.

"I'm starved," Kitty said.

"All right," he said.

He began to gather small deadwood for the stove, and as he stacked the sticks in his arm, he felt almost at peace.

He woke curled in a tight ball, his muscles cramped. His eyes searched for the glow of the cheap alarm; he couldn't remember the day, if he had to work. He felt himself expand, grow briefly enormous, the cabin loft growing with him; then he was looking down at himself, his sitting body, face startled, beside it an unidentifiable lump of blankets he knew was Kitty.

The door to the bedroom was open, the blankets on the swaybacked bed empty. Incredulous, he whipped the blankets off, then bent and peered under the bed, even as he did so realizing the stupidity of the action. He smashed his fist into his palm and cursed, but already there rose in him a grieving relief, such as an athlete might feel at the end of a losing race.

He followed the path to the privy, his legs moving faster with each curse, until he was running. A root tripped him. He rolled and came up on his feet, then stumbled again. He sprawled, his own breath banging harshly in his ears. He lay there until he could hear whippoorwills and the far-off plaint of an owl; he rose and peered into the empty privy, then trotted back to the clearing. He took the car up the road, stopping at boggy spots to search for footprints. When he reached the highway, he drove several miles in both directions, encountering no vehicles, then returned and sat numbly slumped against the steering wheel, listening to the cooling engine, drained of impetus, succumbing to sleep.

He snapped awake, unsure whether he had slept for minutes or hours. A breeze stirred the pines; the moon was high, bright, a crescent, somehow sad in its incompleteness. He ambled down to the water. I'll have to tell her, he thought. Tell her it's over. A lie. From the beginning. He tried to reconstruct the events that seemed to have led to his position there under the high bright moon, somewhere in the eastern Sierra. Maybe it all was meant to happen this way, he thought.

At the end of the dock, wrapped in a blanket, her pale hair catching moonlight, Alice lay curled in sleep. The shock of his weight on the flimsy dock woke her. He stood looking down at what he still perceived as an apparition, suppressing an impulse to embrace her, not out of sensual hunger, but some grave unadmitted compassion evoked by her youth and the seeming fragility of her body.

"I couldn't sleep," Alice said.

The gentle lap of water was punctuated by the cries of an owl. Harry's voice seemed loud: "I wasted a couple of hours, you know that?"

Although her gaze remained intent, she did not appear to hear him.

"I like it here," she said.

"How did you get out?"

"It's so peaceful," she said and turned back to the water. A large bird flew low, skimming the surface, a silhouette against glittering moon-dapple.

"That's what you want to do, isn't it?" she said, and her voice seemed ageless in its serenity. "Isn't it, grasshopper?"

"What?"

"Fly like that. But you don't know where. I don't either. I was really hoping you were somebody important. But—well, it's okay anyway." She paused, then added with paradoxical cheer: "Sometimes I wish I wasn't so smart. You ever wish that?"

He didn't answer. He squatted beside her, and in dreamlike gesture, his hand moved to her hair. Her mouth rose to his, small and hot, and he felt the intense delicateness of her bones conveyed through the kiss. He did not respond, but browsed in amazed stasis, then pulled harshly away. Alice hid her face against her knees. "Shit," she whispered.

"I don't understand," he said, not so much because he didn't but in a weak attempt to soften the blow of his rejection. There was no answer. He tried to touch her. Her shoulders hunched, repelling his hands. When he started to speak again, she turned and for a moment was unrecognizable. The bland youthful planes of her face seemed deepened with a knowing that included pain. It frightened him, and he backed carefully away, his expression drawn in somber bafflement. Then he turned and ran to the cabin and, breathless, climbed into the loft. He crawled under the rough wool blankets, pulling them over his head, gathering the warmth of his own breath. It's trouble, he said. Better if she had gone. Though he longed to touch the woman who lay sleeping beside him, he did not; he was too tainted with confusion. I don't care anymore, he thought. I just don't care.

Her shirt unbuttoned, breasts bare to the sun, Alice lay on the warm wood of the dock. Her feet dangled in the lake and from time to time churned the water with a flurry of kicks, venting her boredom. Kitty sat watching her from the cabin steps, in a confusing haze of admiration and malice, nursing her last cigarette. Then she turned and called to Harry, who sat in the open car, fussing with the radio.

"I'm hungry," she said.

He glanced at her and changed stations.

"Harry, I said I'm hungry. I'm sick of oatmeal."

Then Alice called up from the dock: "Yeah, grasshopper, how about a nice fat lobster for a change?"

Harry whispered a curse.

"Well, how about it?" Kitty said.

"There's no more mention," Harry said.

"No mention?"

"On the radio."

"I thought this was the big time."

"It's good," Harry said. "Maybe he convinced them."

"All this trouble and we don't even make the news," Kitty said.

"It's no goddamn joke."

"Look who's talking," Kitty sneered. "I thought I was the one who took it all too serious. If this is no joke, I'd like to know what is."

"I never said it'd be a goddamn picnic."

"Like hell."

"Ah fuck it," he said and turned the key, pumping the engine into life. He saw Kitty stand, shout, then still holding her cigarette, give chase. Alice joined her. He sped recklessly up the overgrown road. Kitty stopped and he heard her scream: "Don't forget my cigarettes, you bastard! Don't you dare forget. . . ."

The road whipped under him. He was at the edge of control, fighting an impulse to hide in speed, to drive until either he or the machine collapsed. I won't go back, he thought. The goddamn bitch. Goddamn spoiled rotten . . .

The town was dead, imbued with the forlorn complacency of a stifling afternoon. He drove the main drag twice before he stopped at what was the only place open besides the two taverns that marked the east and west boundaries. It was a general store, an ancient adobe structure that still sported a hitchrail. He sat staring at the store, as if it were an apparition; then he became aware of a group of youths leaning against a primer-gray pickup truck a decade old and he felt the onus of the outsider.

The youths stopped talking at the approach of the big white automobile. Harry closed his fist on the pistol, then quickly inserted it into an empty paper sack. He got out, taking the birdcage with him, and entered the shadows of the store, the vacant gazes of the youths falling against his back.

It was a combination hardware-grocery-drug-liquor store, a pandemonium of goods crammed in casual arrangements on the narrow aisles and dangling mazelike from the ceiling. He worked his way to the register where a tall gaunt person of about sixty years stood smoking. When the person spoke, he realized she was a woman, despite the stern mannish lines of her face and the close-cropped white hair and the tuft of whiskers moving on her chin.

"What can I do fer ya?" Her articulation was soft, yet peculiarly precise. Harry felt disarmed, naked; he stammered: "Wondered if you could tell me how far it is to Reno?"

[ 102 ]

The woman pondered for what seemed an excessive time: "Reno?" she said. "Depends how ya drive."

"Normal," he said.

There was another pause. The woman brushed the whiskers on her chin: " 'Bout three hours."

The bird fluttered anxiously around the cage. The woman watched without expression. Overhead the ceiling fans churned the stifling air. Behind him someone stepped into the store and traipsed in heavy boots.

"I'm in kind of a fix," Harry said. "Got to get to Reno to visit my mother. I need a little money. I'd sell you my bird. I'm only asking twenty. You see, he's no ordinary parakeet—"

"Ya don't say," the woman said.

"Cost over sixty," Harry said. "I'd buy him back for thirty in less than a week. It'd be like a deposit. I really don't want to sell him."

The woman picked up a smoldering cigarette from a tin ashtray and inhaled deeply, exhaling through her nostrils. She mashed the stub between her fingers, shredding the tobacco.

"Got no need of any songbird, mister."

"No, it's just a loan," Harry said. "The bird is security."

The woman shook her head.

"He's worth a lot more than twenty. The cage is worth that."

"Thanks anyway."

The customer who had entered after him came to the counter with a pack of beer under either arm; he was a heavy, lumbering, weathered man, with years of desert on his face.

"Maybe Mr. Trapper here would like a bird." She cackled with sudden secret mirth, and the man laughed with her.

"He tryin' to hawk you that bird, Miss Mabel?"

The woman shrugged. "Says he's tryin' ta see his ma up in Reno. Reckon the closest hockshop's there too." The man and woman guffawed together in easy good humor, then the man suggested: "Hell, try Smitty over at the Shell station. He might be loco enough to swap you that bird for a tank of gas.

Had him a crow once." He laughed remembering. "Taught that blamed crow to curse." Miss Mabel and Trapper again laughed.

"Well, tell you the truth, I'm hungry," Harry said. "I got enough gas."

"Well, stranger, wouldn't take you but two or three hours to get up to Reno."

There was a silence. He made no attempt to twist his story into something that would explain his need for food. Then Miss Mabel lit another cigarette and he realized his questioners had accepted his lie and had no use to uncover it further. Harry shuffled, wanting to blurt out his gratitude. He felt the weight of the pistol inside the paper sack and wanted to hide it, still afraid of what he might in desperation do. Then, as if the woman had read his thought, she gestured toward his left hand and asked with casual curiosity, "What's in the sack, mister?" And because they had not probed his life, he felt a need to satisfy this more immediate curiosity. He set the sack on the counter. The woman showed no particular surprise at its contents.

"A handsome firearm, mister. I'd loan ya fifty on it. Ten percent a week. Give ya a month to claim it."

Harry shook his head.

"It's my father's. I promised never to let it go."

The man picked up the pistol and looked at it, nodded his approval. He took out his wallet and extended to Harry two fifty-dollar bills. Harry shook his head.

"I couldn't."

"How much you want fer it?" the woman said.

"I can't sell it?"

"What ya need it fer, mister?"

"It's my father's."

"Ya ain't goin' ta make no trouble around here?"

"No. God no," Harry said.

"Maybe he's got a grudge against a casino up in Reno," the man said laughing.

Harry smiled. The woman nodded and with a slow contemplative gesture stuck a fresh cigarette in the corner of her mouth. She lit it with a wooden match struck with her thumbnail.

"All right," she said. "How much ya want fer the bird?" She spoke so casually he did not immediately react.

"The bird?"

"How much?"

"Twenty," he said.

"Twenty in credit okay?"

"I'll buy him back for thirty next week. I promise. Want me to write it?"

The woman waved her hand at him, dismissing the proposal.

"Can it talk?"

"He can learn," Harry said. "Really he can." Harry whistled and the bird mimicked. The woman grinned, the cigarette dangling precariously. "All right, mister. Take what you need up to twenty bucks."

Harry started with a box of ammunition.

Nathaniel Fisk stepped out onto the veranda of his rustic cottage at the Halcyon Days Retreat and cursed softly into the ocean breeze that had rustled up through the narrow canyon from the beach a half-mile below. The senator's curse carried a smell of scotch and cigar and a hint of fear. The rustle of live oak and eucalyptus brought no comfort, nor the mauve and pink sunset washing on the haze. The cottage, which had served as his personal sanctuary for twenty years, was now besieged by the Federal Bureau of Investigation. The senator glanced down at the gray automobile sitting in the shadows, its front doors open to the evening air. One of the men was reading a comic book. The other sat smoking, apparently listening to a piece of classical piano music the senator identified as composed by Satie. The man listening waved.

"Satie?" the senator called in his voice of practiced amicability.

"Yes, sir. Beautiful evening, isn't it, sir? Considering the circumstances of course."

The senator nodded and to avoid further conversation returned to the interior of the cottage. He glanced at the beige telephone sitting imperially beside the bronze statue of the Spirit of St. Louis and regretted ever having allowed its installation. It was strange how a simple device could remind him of so many irritations, the most potent being his earlier conversation with Vincent Riley, the bureau's station chief, during which the senator had requested the removal of the tap. Of course the reaction had been predictable, but he had given Cloud his word, so he had at least to go through with it to keep his conscience clear. And part of him so resented the bureau's intrusion that he secretly welcomed any excuse to rankle them. Riley had assumed his most patronizing tone and explained: "These people are absolutists, senator. They only understand the very elements they themselves employ—terror and subterfuge."

"Damn it, Riley, he's not what you think," Fisk had answered. "He's really rather—" The senator censored himself, appalled by his irrational impulse to defend the criminal who had instigated this insane incident. So the conversation ended without him having gained a foothold of respect; in fact, he had worsened his position. In the afternoon he was informed the bureau had been unable to trace Cloud's second call; they suspected it derived from outside the state, which tended to confirm their fears about a terrorist cadre. This information was conveyed by Smith, who still sat guard in the gray sedan.

Later he talked to his wife, who in a state of sedated hysteria asked him to do something about the barrage of press waiting for news of what they were supposed not to even know. The senator sent his aide Roland Thompson, who made a short statement declaring Alice Fisk's abduction was a "groundless rumor." When the press demanded to know the girl's whereabouts, Thompson stated she was "attending a special tennis school in England."

The whole affair had taken on an abstract quality, generated by its very unbelievability. It seemed an insulting plot in an unlikely melodrama that was beneath the senator's dignity. The issue was further confused by his ambivalence toward the federal authorities, and what was even more incomprehensible, his ambivalence toward the man who called himself Cloud. It was entirely unlike the senator to be ambivalent about anything, especially a grotesque breach of the law. Although he bordered on vanity in regard to his tolerance —in part because it was hard won from an essentially rigid nature—, he was a man who worshipped common sense and he was certain Cloud's act lacked any modicum of that. He found himself chewing cigar after cigar, his tongue bitter, his mouth watering against the smoke. Worse, he was drinking from early afternoon on, though he had managed to preserve the illusion of sobriety.

Late Friday afternoon he drove down the hill and took a walk along his private beach, accompanied by Smith, who stated with deadly earnestness: "They might be watching, waiting for an opportunity to make an attempt on your life."

Exhausted beyond protest, the senator simply grumbled: "If the press hasn't found me, I'll be damned if Cloud ever could."

The walk did not comfort him. He returned to the cottage and sat gloomily before the unnecessary fire and watched the sunset fall to deep indigo.

The telephone jolted him from half-sleep. He knew it was Cloud. Another small-time dreamer, dreaming the big time. The senator almost smiled. Perhaps he could put him straight, convince him to give up before it got completely beyond control. The telephone rang again. Hastily he picked up, and before he realized what he was saying, Fisk informed Cloud that he had ordered the tap off, but was certain it was still there, that if he told where the drop was to take place, the authorities would surely intervene.

"But you know I'm going to hold her for twenty-four hours after anyway. We agreed to that."

"I trust you, Cloud. But nobody trusts me. I want this over with. I want Allie released unharmed."

"We've got to trust each other."

"That's what I'm saying. Exactly what I'm saying." Fisk's words did not feel like his own, yet he did not sense they were hypocritical, and the senator had always prided himself on knowing exactly when he was lying.

[ 108 ]

There was a static-filled pause, and Cloud began to speak in a low nervous rush: "Your daughter is fine, but I can't be responsible if they try something. You've got to convince them to stay out of it. It's got to be clean, you understand?"

The senator gave the number of his local office and told him to leave his instructions on the answering device.

"But how will I know—"

"Leave your instructions and my man will get the tape before they can. Cloud, you've got to see my position. They're listening right now."

"I can't afford all these calls."

"Call collect, for christ's sake! Now call me back in an hour and I'll confirm that I've got your instructions."

"How do I know this isn't a goddamn ploy?"

"The senator sighed. "You don't, my boy. You just plain don't."

"If you try anything, you know what'll happen."

"I believe you, Cloud. I do believe you."

It was Smith who knocked on the door. The senator did not answer. He was sweating, weak, baffled by his own conspiracy.

From outside the agent's voice pleaded for him to open. The senator made a call to Roland Thompson and told him to seize the tape, and under no circumstances to allow anyone to hear it. The barrage of knocks continued. Finally Fisk let the agent in. Smith was obviously perplexed by the senator's defiant course, and glanced at him shyly, embarrassed to face an esteemed man's transgression.

"I don't think you needed to go that far, sir. But it was convincing."

"We do need his complete trust, don't we?"

"But admitting the tap—well, perhaps you're right, sir. Now, how exactly will we get the tape, sir?"

"You don't have to worry about that, Mr. Smith. Mr. Thompson will deliver it directly to Mr. Riley."

"But sir—"

"Please, Mr. Smith. I'd like a little privacy. If that isn't against the bureau's sacred duty."

"Of course not, sir, but I feel—"

"Would you kindly leave me in peace, Mr. Smith."

The man nodded and left. The senator slumped into his chair trembling with spent rage. A dull pain radiated from his chest through his left shoulder. He took a drink directly from the bottle. More than anything he wanted to sleep.

Kitty and Alice sat beside each other on the cabin steps, their postures relaxed, even friendly, so from a distance they might have appeared as intimate friends or sisters. But at close range the older woman's face revealed a grim fretting, while Alice appeared guileless, compassionate, open, as though she had abandoned all jealous competition for the absent Harry.

They sat and watched the sun sink below the line of trees. The heat of the day dissipated and the cool of twilight brought a forlornness, the little death of a day. Simultaneously the women felt the expanse of hours rush irrevocably into the past; they looked at each other, and for a moment they hovered on the edge of impulsive embrace. It was Kitty who turned away.

"I'm sorry about all this," she said.

Alice shrugged. "Don't feel bad."

"I do." Kitty moved rapidly away, stumbling on the stairs, her face bent into her hands. She rushed headlong down to the dock, and jumped into a rough wood skiff they had found earlier in the day and dragged on a pair of logs to the water. After a time, Alice went down to the skiff and tried to comfort the woman.

"He'll come back," Alice said.

"I don't care," Kitty said. "It's not him I care about."

Alice reached to touch her, but when Kitty felt the girl's hand, she shrank, uttering a small cry.

"He'll be back," Alice said simply.

The light suddenly went purple and dusky. The woods moved close. The twilight hush gave way and the night birds began to make their noise. Alice thought of home, but if there was any longing, it was simply habit. She remembered how she had dreamed of living in the woods, her only companions wild creatures. She had read *Green Mansions* over and over, luxuriating in its jungle romance. She had hallucinated intimacies with wild animals. But some streak of stubborn pragmatism had sabotaged the romance until now when the universe of the woods overwhelmed her with its actuality and she realized her earlier trepidations about being alone in the forest had been a convention, an assumption. She welcomed the darkness, the mystery of the breeze stirring the pines. I want to stay, she thought. And with the ease of youth, she repudiated all past dreams, all the prestige of her circle. It was a marvelous bright feeling, and she longed to tell someone. Yes, her decision was momentous enough to deserve an audience. But before she could tell the woman, perhaps even request she stay and be her companion and friend, the woods were invaded by a pair of headlamps. Then came the breath of the familiar engine, and the white automobile like a phantom floating through the trees.

Harry squinted against the scent of the spirit gum, then with trembling fingers stuck the mustache in place. He sat on the edge of the basin and examined himself at close range in the mirror. He decided to darken his eyebrows. A jet screamed overhead, shaking the motel. A few seconds later its engines reversed as the plane touched down at Reno's municipal airport. The noise was replaced by the chatter of the television set in the adjacent room where Alice lay sprawled in drugged obliteration, guarded by Kitty's nervous pacing.

This was the second time he had assumed the disguise, the first being immediately after its purchase a year before when he had gone walking in the downtown Sunday crowds, mostly Latins and blacks and dispossessed whites populating another world. He had felt the change in his gait, how his shoulders of their own assumed a certain proud rigidity, how easily he had smiled, even speaking pleasantries to strange women. But after that, though tempted by the confidence the disguise bestowed, he had avoided it.

He took a drink from the pint bottle, now almost empty, and thought of his bird and the tall gaunt woman's sudden reversal, in the end offering him ten dollars in cash in addition to the goods; again he was overwhelmed by a sense of destiny, of the strange interconnectedness of things. He shivered, feeling a rush of fear. Another jet passed over, reminding him of his appointment, and again he drank. In the mirror he could see Kitty pacing, could feel her manic aliveness. Maybe never see her again. Never touch. He armed himself with deliberate calm, no more substantial than the mustache he wore. Suddenly she broke into shrieking laughter, directed at the disguise. Unperturbed, as if her outburst were a physical tic he was long accustomed to, he handed her the bottle. She drank quickly, spilling whiskey over her face, while he knotted his tie and rolled his shoulders into his jacket. His appearance was sinister but comic, an image even he recognized: the thrift-store gangster, the criminal with the substance of a celluloid image—yet had he not come to believe that crime *did* pay? He was a man without capital, a nobody. So he had to wing it, to keep moving on his own thin ice. He snickered. The disguise only accentuated his convoluted thoughts. Even now, he knew terror might seize him completely, that he might simply abandon himself to cowardice and drive until he was exhausted, caught, and then perhaps he would take the last refuge: madness.

He saw her in the mirror, bottle lifted. Their eyes met. Slowly Kitty took the bottle from her lips. A softness entered her face, an innocence, as if she had shed ten years. He had witnessed this shedding before, mistaken it for affection, even what he thought might be called love: she seemed to look at him for the first time, truly look and see beyond his capacity to see his own self. He wanted to prolong this moment, as a lover wanting to prolong the threshold of climax.

"You're handsome," she whispered.

He did not move or speak, afraid she would flinch and the spell be broken.

"You look so calm," she whispered in soft amazement.

He felt a swelling pride; her whisper had touched his blood, and her words annealed his disguise into invincible armor.

"In an hour," she whispered, "in an hour we'll have it." Then she was against him, her mouth raw with cigarettes and whiskey, inviting with ravening fierceness. Why only now, at the last second, had she opened herself: did she sense some disastrous outcome? Or was she simply fearful he would betray her and not return? He heard her voice again, soft, without accusation: "Harry, it's going to happen, it's real, isn't it?"

"I never thought it wasn't."

It was she who led him now, just as it was she who had decided, the night of their departure from Los Angeles, to take him in her mouth. She's gone mad, he thought. It's not me she wants. Anyone.

"I've got to go," he said.

"I want you," she whispered.

"Later."

"Harry, I'm all hot inside."

"Maybe you're scared."

"Aren't you?"

"Sure."

"But I'm not bored. Not bored at all."

He snickered. "That's nice."

"You think I'm crazy. You think underneath everything I'm just crazy."

"It's all crazy."

"Harry, I'm sorry. I've been such a bitch."

"It's just nerves."

"But I've been awful."

"No. That's not true."

"Harry, you really are special. I see it now. And I know it'll be good between us—it will—once we get the money it'll be different."

"Sure. But I gotta go to get it—gotta meet that son of a bitch."

"You're scared."

"Sure."

"You think he kept his word?"

"I don't know. If I'm not back in an hour, just leave."

"With what? A lousy five bucks."

"I'll be back," he said.

"I know," she said and she pulled him to her, and reaching into his trousers she took him in her hand and fiercely tried to thrust him inside her.

"I'm so hot," she whispered.

"I got to go."

"Oh god," she said. "I'm just so hot."

He pulled away from her. She whimpered as if hurt.

"It's okay. It'll be okay."

Suddenly she took him by the shoulders and shook him. "Do you realize?" she said, as if she had at that moment herself recognized something monstrous beyond words. "Don't you realize what we're doing?"

"I'll be back," he said.

He locked the door and moved into the stifling twilight. Neon burned against a deepening sky. He moved now with unusual grace, like a creature possessed with purpose. He became part of the automobile, part of the very noise of Reno's dusk. The streetlamps came on. He had no thought of the woman left weeping, or the girl in her drugged slumber. No thought of past or future or consequence or danger. A tune sprung into his head, and he lifted his harmonica. He reached the Western Airlines desk just as the flight bearing a blue-gray Samsonite luggage case was touching down.

Roland Thompson, a young man going places, was drunk; his drunkenness was disconcerting because he did not know how it had happened and felt no responsibility for it. He ran along the echoing marble corridor of the terminal, the suitcase banging against his leg. He stumbled and skidded headlong. Several faces poked down, then someone extended a hand. He stood and moved on, plagued by a grim sense of accelerating time and impending disaster. Then he stopped. His forehead was cold with sweat. He felt sticky, soiled. This was all quite different from what he had expected.

The message was waiting at the information desk. He looked to see if anyone was following. He saw no one.

He went outside as the message instructed, entered a taxi, gave the driver the name of a coffee shop. He noticed a large white convertible with its top up, but it didn't look like an undercover car. He fixated on several other vehicles, but each would pass or turn off. Even the white convertible disappeared.

Although he had been in the cab less than ten minutes, he had the impression he had been traveling at tremendous speed for hours. He still had no idea when his destination would be reached. He clutched the suitcase as if it were trying to leave him. Suddenly, in wild fear, he imagined a band of guerrillas armed with rifles standing around him, questioning, firing at his feet in jeering celebration.

The taxi pulled into a parking lot. Thompson sat transfixed, his eyes roving frantically from car to car. Somewhere here, more than likely, the federal agents were lurking, waiting for the right moment.

"This is it, mister. The Magpie Coffee Shop."

"Just wait," Thompson said, handing the cabbie an extra bill.

"What for?"

"I just want you to wait."

"Listen buddy, I got another call."

"I'm meeting someone. Maybe they won't show," Thompson said. He opened the door, but still did not get out. His legs had gone limp. "I'm afraid," he said with blank amazement. He caught a glimpse of himself in the rearview mirror, his face twisted into a grin. He had no idea who or what he was grinning for; perhaps he thought someone intending to shoot him down would have doubts about shooting a man who was smiling.

He was standing, still grinning, outside the car. A horn blared at him and a door swung open. It was the white convertible. A man with a mustache, a panama hat, and white suit told him to get into the car. He reminds me of someone, someone I knew in high school, Thompson thought. Then he was inside. The car lurched, pressing the suitcase into his chest.

"Just calm down," the man said.

Thompson realized the smirk was still on his face, and his mouth was stammering something; he was trying to ask the man if they had gone to the same high school.

"See this," the man said, and flashed a large pistol; it seemed to Thompson excessively shiny, maybe a toy. He began to think he should assault the man, that he might come out a hero.

"My name's Thompson," he blurted.

"Okay, Thompson. Just don't get funny. If I don't arrive where we're going in ten minutes, something bad will happen to her."

"Don't worry," Thompson said. "We don't want any trouble."

With a sudden squalling of tires, the car turned off the boulevard onto a residential side street and pulled to the curb.

"Open it," the man said.

"What?"

"The suitcase. Open it."

Thompson started to feel in his pockets for the key; the man jammed the pistol into his ribs. In panic Thompson thrust up his hands.

"What in hell?" the man said.

"The key," Thompson explained.

The man frisked him and found the key. Thompson unlocked the suitcase, keeping his eye on the gun, thinking, It's not real, I don't believe it.

The money was wrapped in paper packets denoting the amount. The man glanced briefly, with no apparent emotion. Even to Thompson the money had an unreal quality, like a photograph.

"Close it," the man said.

After that the man drove calmly, humming along with the radio. Occasionally the man grinned, as if at some private joke. Thompson began to wonder if the man had forgotten him, and once again contemplated heroic acts.

"It's been almost ten minutes," Thompson said.

"Don't worry," the man said.

"Isn't your name Cloud?"

"Yes. Doctor Cloud."

"You're an M.D.?"

"Doctor of Philosophy."

"Funny thing for a man of your education—"

"There's lots of funny things," the man said.

They stopped at a light. Thompson studied the man, trying to memorize his features. He convinced himself that the threat to Alice was a bluff. He wanted to jump the man. He was waiting for the moment. There was always the right

[ *119* ]

moment for these things. He knew that much.

But the right moment never seemed to come, and Thompson began to worry something absurd might happen, that the man was more than he seemed. He had been around politics long enough to know how to play that game.

Before Thompson could find the right moment for heroism, the car was parked by a rear unit of a cinderblock motel. The man ordered him out, then nudged him along a coral pink walkway. On one side of the walk was a desolate strip of cactus, among which stood several cracked plaster flamingos; but even as he noted these details, Thompson felt peculiarly dazed, as if he had been drugged with a substance to disperse and confound memory.

A woman opened the door to the man's knock. She was a shopworn twenty or a youthful thirty, he could not be sure. She had a heavy crimson mouth and black eyebrows, fluffy ash-blond hair: a wig perhaps. Again he was not sure. But of one thing he was certain: she had the demeanor of a callgirl. Though he had no direct experience with such women, she seemed to fulfill the characteristics he knew such women would have.

"This is Mr. Thompson," the man said. "The man who brought us the money."

"Glad to meet you," Thompson said, and offered his hand. The woman nodded an acknowledgment, then turned away and lit another cigarette from the butt end of the one she had in her mouth. Thompson strained to note the brand. The woman whispered something to the man, who nodded and pointed to the suitcase. The woman stared at it, then knelt and touched it, almost embracing it.

"Sit down," the man said. "Over there."

Thompson did as he was told. For the first time he noticed another woman, no more than a girl, asleep on the bed. The man said: "You can see she's unharmed. We'll wake her in a minute."

"What now?"

The man smiled. "We leave and you stay."

"You said you'd contact him."

"Not from here."

"He wants to speak with Alice," Thompson said and again glanced at the sleeping girl; he had not seen her for two years and did not remember her.

"We'll call around nine tonight, just as we planned."

The woman opened the suitcase: her breath drew in, then she broke into giggles which she muffled in her hands.

"Close it," the man said.

The woman stopped laughing. Thompson was no longer afraid; part of him was convinced he could get up and walk out of the motel room and no harm would befall Alice or himself. Yet he did not move. And a few seconds later he had no choice: the man had shackled his wrists to the arms of the chair. Then his ankles were bound with lamp cord, the man working in subdued frenzy, while the woman held the gun. Thompson closed his eyes and prayed. Once the woman broke into giggles that weaved unsteadily on the brink of hysteria. The man hissed at her to shut up.

They woke Alice, who blinked, then fell back to sleep. They kept shaking her and slapping her. Finally the woman brought a wet washcloth and squeezed it over the girl's face.

"You can talk to her now," the man said.

Thompson heard himself asking the obvious questions. Alice's answers were groggy, without interest: yes she was all right, no they had not mistreated her, yes they would let her go. After this brief interview, the man placed the gun against Thompson's temple and ordered him to open his mouth. Oh my god, they're going to kill me. He tried to scream.

"Open it," the man said, and the muzzle bored into Thompson's skull. The woman stood before him with a roll of tissue paper. The man nodded and the woman began to stuff wads of paper into his mouth. Instinctively Thompson tried to spit. Again the pistol dug in. The room seemed too bright, and he was aware of the man's breath: sour, metallic.

"Relax," the man said. "Just relax."

The man handed the gun to the woman and bound Thompson's mouth with a nylon stocking. Suddenly the room was quiet. The three people facing him were transfixed, listening to something. At first Thompson could only hear the throbbing of his own skull, then he became aware of a remote thumping coming through the wall. The thumping increased, and then came a harsh drawn-out crying, whether of pleasure or pain it was impossible to determine.

"Well I'll be damned," the man said.

A jet passed overhead, its engine screaming. The man moved: he opened the suitcase, took a packet of twenties, peeled off two, and left them on the nightstand. Then he moved to the television set and angled it to face Thompson.

"Which channel you want?"

The man began to switch through the channels. The second time around, Thompson nodded his choice.

"We want to thank you," the man said. "Good luck to you." The man spoke without irony. Then the woman blew him a kiss and Alice waved good-bye. The door closed and he heard the lock turn. Thompson sat for half an hour in dazed trance, making vain attempts to free himself. He was trying to keep all the significant details alive, knowing his testimony would be essential. But already most of what had happened seemed like a dispersing dream. All he could think was how wrinkled his suit was and how his muscles ached. A quiet fury rose up in him. Why didn't I jump him when I had the chance?

At a town called Minden they dragged her out of a heavy slumber, insisting she talk to her father. As she stood in sullen half-sleep, rubbing her arms against the cold, he dialed from a booth in the corner of a service-station lot. She heard him say, "You can speak to your daughter" and then felt the receiver, cold and heavy as iron, against her face. She heard the familiar voice, the calm and serene patriarch, a bit weary and aloof.

"Are you all right, Allie?"

She nodded, unable to speak.

"Alice?"

"I'm fine." The words struggled out, furry, remote.

"They haven't hurt you?"

"No."

"Well, it's been quite an ordeal. But it's over. I think I can trust him to release you."

Again she nodded.

"Alice, do you hear me?"

"Yes, Daddy," she said and felt her eyes warm and her whole being begin to soften. Don't, she said, don't give in— but already she was crumbling into regressive childhood, wanting to curl up, to bawl out to him, O Daddy, Daddy, I'm so alone and scared and nowhere to go.

"Do you hear me, Alice?"

"Yes, Daddy."

"Can I take these people at their word?"

"Yes."

"They have the money?"

"Yes. They're real happy about it. They keep saying how much they appreciate—"

"Fine. I'm so glad. And Roland?"

"Who?"

"Roland Thompson."

"They tied him up. He's okay."

"Are these people revolutionaries, terrorists—what are they?"

There was a pause. "I'm not sure. They're just people I guess."

"Well stress to them I've given my word. I won't go back on it."

"Yes, Daddy."

"They said they'd give you fare home. You have this number?"

"Yes."

"Is there anything you need to tell me, daughter, that perhaps you can't?"

"No, I guess not."

"I'm sure you'll be stronger for all this, Allie. You know we love you."

"I'm sure you're right, Daddy."

"Is Cloud there?"

"Yes."

"Let me speak with him."

Harry took the phone and spoke in friendly tones for several minutes: their conspiratorial camaraderie disgusted her. But he's just protecting himself, she said. Or thinks he is. He doesn't know my father. But I forgive you, grasshopper. I forgive you.

"He seems like an all-right guy," Harry said.

"Sure, until you get to know him."

"I don't aim to."

"Me neither. Not any more than I've already had to."

They ambled back to the car, where Kitty sat huddled in her coat, eyeing them coldly. Alice wanted to offer a few friendly words, but nothing came to mind. She climbed into the back and lay gazing at the stars. Her hands moved under the blanket, then her right hand moved inside her underwear to touch herself, the touches casual, almost innocent of erotic intent. It was something to do. What if I really don't go back? she thought.

Kitty smoked and fidgeted, thinking of the blue-gray Samsonite in the trunk, wishing she could again run her hands over the neat packets of bills, could smell, touch, devour them. She lit another cigarette and glanced at him, wondering what he thought. His face betrayed nothing: he seemed utterly intent on the road, keeping the big car just under the limit, slowing for the small desert towns, heading south, back to the known sanctuary. She studied his face, intense, hawklike, with its lines of suppressed fury—and now, at this moment, she again saw him as handsome, and a primitive flush of desire moved in her. He was handsome, even with the ridiculous mustache, and he looked younger, as if something had been lifted from him, some of the rage.

He turned toward her, and she looked away, annoyed at his sensitivity to her gaze. And the way he smiled: almost obscene with affection. She cringed, wondering for the hundredth time how she had fallen in with him.

"You cold?" he said.

She shook her head, feeling the taint of hypocrisy in her own smile; she wrapped tighter in her coat, sinking deeper into its soft animal shell. She felt immensely small, so small and insignificant even the thought of the fabled sum in the trunk gave no comfort. There was no one. No one who really loved her—except him. This Harry. It did not seem possible, this injustice, after the many times she had lent herself to strangers.

All she wanted to do was sleep. Perhaps if she could sleep long enough, it would right itself, the madness disperse. She saw herself asleep on a beach of white sand, her feet basking in tropical water, a safe empty beach where no man would accost her.

The change in vibrations woke her. She sat up, then saw him in the hard glare of the headlamps removing the crosspoles from the wooden barrier. Suddenly she felt intensely awake, piqued by an abstract distress, as if the machinery of the law were transmitting its demand for revenge through the air itself.

"What's the matter?"

"Nothing," she said.

"In a few minutes we can rest."

The car jolted along the overgrown road, shadowy apparitions leaping out of the rich undergrowth. She felt an ambush waiting at the clearing, but she did not dare warn him. He parked; the engine died; she clung to him, terrified.

"It's all right," he said. "We did it. We're home free."

They left Alice sleeping in the back seat and walked to the cabin. She felt another moment of terror as he opened the door. He lit the kerosene lamp, then brought out his wallet and took from it a flattened hand-rolled cigarette.

"For the celebration," he said. "Topnotch stuff."

She smiled despite herself. "You're such a goof."

"I know," he said. He struck a match. She bent to the flame, sucked the smoke deeply in, felt an instantaneous rush of comfort anticipating the glaze of intoxication. He made a fire, then with a jaunty bow he left to return to the car. As soon as he had gone, her chest swelled with emotion: she had a vision of him saving, always saving, waiting for the precious future moment. She felt caught in his sadness, felt maybe she too had been always waiting, postponing, afraid to commit herself—and now that she had, it was accidental and mad, doomed to failure.

He came back and hefted the weighty suitcase into the loft. When he found her there crying, he did not ask why, he

[ *127* ]

simply held her, seeming to know better why she wept than she did. Then, for no reason, the tears broke into laughing, long weepy trills of baffling laughter. She opened the suitcase, and in the smoking yellow light of the lamp, the packets of bills wavered like a mirage. She reached and touched. She snatched up a packet, tore off the paper band, and showered the bills into the air. By some sleight of hand, or hallucination, a bottle of champagne appeared. She laughed again as he pulled forth provisions he had purchased while she slept. It was a banquet. He fed her, drunkenly placing bits of cheese or snippets of sardine on her extended tongue. Her intoxication was complete. She laughed: I've never seen him before, never really seen him until now. A low rumble came from the charged air, and the cabin shook. For a moment they froze, silent, waiting, the shudder of thunder moving in their blood like some final urge to drunkenness. The first drops fell, then quickly swelled into a terrible alive thudding. Kitty touched the roof, the vibrations thrilling her hands. They drank, toasted, tore open the neat packets loosing more money to rain down onto the dusty mattress that had held them for two chaste nights.

He descended from the loft to restoke the fire and she tossed a handful of bills after him. One caught in a draft and swirled into the fire, ignited, and swirled back into the room, floated in flame, then dropped in ash. In that instant the whole fragility of existence came over her, a desolate stab to her jubilance. Then he was back in the loft, his face close. She began to feel quite lost and insubstantial. The rain roared. A blue flash illumined the cabin—then came the crack and roll and boom, the shudders seeming to loose in her a wild surge of energy: the storm was inside her, and she saw on his face a determined lust rising through what had always been to her an expression of slovenly infatuation. His mouth opened and she felt he would curse; and she felt her own mouth open to ask: "Why? What have I done?" Then, without utterance, she sensed a meaning to his curse; it was the curse of the poet for his muse. His fierceness moved toward her, his whole body shaking, raging at his own tenderness, his own love for her. She sensed this in a split second of insight filled with the rage of rain and the turbulent sighing of trees. Her mind began to move in a frantic chant: *Please don't hurt please don't hurt*—yet despite the turmoil, part of her felt calm, even expectant. Then he was on her, his mouth hard against hers. She resisted, trying to speak through his kisses. She wanted to tell him about the dance she saw: they were at the mercy of the blood's storm, about to do what men and women do, have done, yet not because they willed it, or even desired it, but because some force drove them to it. Her laughter smothered in his mouth, and she feared he would hit her, mistaking its meaning.

He did not hit her. He rose on one elbow and seemed to speak, but she heard only the racket of rain and wind and thunder. He opened his belt, all the time holding her with his eyes. She found herself thrilled by his fury. He was exposed, his erection jutting absurdly between brass zipper teeth. Now she felt a quiver of fear, perhaps at its sheer size and aggressiveness—yet at the center of the storm she knew an unresisting calm was ready to take him.

She stared with an expression of passive indifference, hiding her desire. He ripped away the last barriers of her clothing while she lay limp as a doll. His eyes flicked over her skin and she could feel them burning her. He pushed her legs apart, a ruthless exposing of her tenderest and most secret part. He was over her, a fierce animal. In one slow inexorable thrust he entered.

Her breath tightened at the invasion: it was so hot, like a hot stone forcing her to acknowledge her own soft vulnerability. Now she knew there was no choice but to abandon herself. She was helplessly pinned under his thrusts, his body heavy, hard, bruising.

Then she became aware of his thrusts going beyond his control, beyond the want even to satisfy her. She sensed too that her indifference had forced the full rage of his desire, and this rage had kept him from coming too quickly. She found herself watching the heave of his back, the almost ridiculous butting of his haunches. It was ridiculous and yet strangely lovely, a kind of dance; she could put her mind in either place, though it seemed the ridiculous had the stronger pull. Her observations gave her a peculiar pleasure: it was the pleasure of the actress in her that knew she could provoke his climax with a few cries of feigned rapture. She felt sorry for him. One minute he was raping her, but all she had to do was yield and he was again at her mercy. She listened to his hard furious breath, urging her open. But still she did not relinquish herself. She watched him. Then before she had expected, his cry came in her ears, like the cry of a small wounded creature, and she felt his seeds spring. He held fast to her and did not slip away. Then he began to thrust again, slowly plunging into his own seed, trying to find her, the soft center, wanting to crawl inside her.

But he could not continue. He softened and began to go small. She felt his body shake and realized he was weeping: it was as if she had vanquished him.

She lay under him, torn between holding him and pushing him away. His tender weakness left her in confused immobility. She dozed. Then she woke, feeling a rush of cool wind and a loud roar of rain. She was afraid. Her fear woke him, and in seconds he was hard again and slipping into her.

He did not move, simply lay, his hard potency deep inside her. It was as if he had rooted himself in her for good. It began to frighten her, the way her desire rose to him. But he would not let her move, and in the forced stillness she felt a threat, something far more unmanageable than the previous assault. A guttural wail moved up from her middle. She stopped it in her throat. Then her body seemed to give way, and a hotness sprung in her center, a heat she had never felt before. She became molten, breathing, caressing the hardness that now began to stir, withdrawing ever so slightly, then plunging softly, deeper. She uttered a cry, a long wailing sigh and she was gone. She wanted to swallow him, pull him in, feel the fierce tenderness of his sex, its vulnerability equal to her own, doomed to live in brief spells, then die and live again, doomed to sadness with each pleasure, always alone, always seeking the soft home. It was this tenderness she felt plunge into her and turn her molten beyond the point of turning back. She had never let herself be here before; the fire ran through her belly, driving her hips, her feet pushing the scattered gray and green bills that littered the bed. The fire became sound, a long whining, half protest, half exclamation of surprise. Her belly moved in excruciating waves, soft shuddering convulsions she could not stop, and the fire broke into moaning and cracked into lesser shudders that were her own helpless weeping of surrender.

He rested still on top of her. The rain beat on the roof, but softer now. She was aware the light had changed, the fire died to coals. He was quiet inside her, softly iridescent, asleep; she was glad he was asleep, glad he had not noticed her weeping, or if he had, had not questioned. Then her mind rebelled, rose up with a paradoxical anger that this stranger had brought her to feel what she had never felt before, dumbly, blindly, breaking her resistance with his fierce tenderness. She wanted to tell someone, wanted to be home, to be someplace safe, away from all confusion. She tried to think of such a place: she saw the open stage, the clouds of costumed dancers in rigorous and unified formality, herself among them, suddenly lifted by strong supple arms into the spotlight.

She pulled from under him and tugged the rough wool blankets over them, and lying there on the dusty mattress on the loose money, she let her mind drift into quietness on the rain.

Below a figure moved. Alice's pale towhead caught the light from the shower of sparks as she dumped another log on the fire.

[ *131* ]

The sun was already high when Harry woke and crawled out of the damp mound of blankets, ten- and twenty-dollar bills plastered to his skin. His head was muzzy, his focus scattered; his stomach rumbled. He rubbed his hand across five days of stubble. Even in sleep Kitty's face seemed troubled. He touched her forehead, trying to impart tenderness, peace. The memory of the shudders and the sighing belly sound evoked fresh desire, and he wanted to plunge into her and again lose himself.

He slapped his fist into his palm, thrilled, proud, frisky; his head went under the blanket. She turned from him, still sleeping. For a moment he was struck with a sense of brutal rejection, but it dispersed instantly—she was simply asleep.

He went outside, his step jaunty. He began to whistle. Then he spotted Alice: she lay naked on the dock, a nymph, already the lean body browning. Even asleep she exuded a sort of natural proprietorship that appeared to derive from the very glitter of the water, from the sun on her slowly rising and falling belly. He stood one step from the dock and spoke to her, informing her they were to leave in an hour. Not the slightest flicker crossed her face; there was only the lapping of water and the faint stirring of pines, the whisper of a car passing on the highway a mile to the south.

"Alice, we got to get ready," he said.

"I heard you last night," she said. "Sounded pretty good."

A hot flush swept his face. She smirked, then rolled over, her high hard rump bearing the imprint of weathered wood.

He watched the imprint fade. He had no idea how long he had stared at her.

"What?" he muttered.

She murmured a lazy reply. "You heard me. And I wouldn't mind . . ."

"Mind what?"

"Some of the same."

"You're going home."

"You didn't answer me."

"There's nothing to answer, Alice. I want you ready in ten minutes."

"Don't worry," she said and raised her hand, her middle finger extended in repudiation. He walked back to the cabin kicking at the soft loamy earth.

When next he looked she was halfway down the lake, a tiny blur of movement rowing the heavy skiff. He ran to the end of the dock and yelled; his voice returned, a faint mocking echo. He tore along a rudimentary trail that followed the south shore. In a few hundred yards the trail disintegrated completely and he simply crashed into the undergrowth, which tore at him as if in communion with the girl's mockery. Suddenly the ground sank from under him. He was in a bog formed by the lake spreading into a low southward curve invisible from the cabin. Dead trees brooded around him, silvery gray. The air churned with insects. He called out, his voice echoing dismally.

It took him half an hour to circle the bog. By then he was too exhausted to hold onto his fury. The woods now were open, easy walking, and gradually the remote lazy serenity of the day began to seep into him. He stopped and drank from a spring, the water burning cold.

He found the skiff at the far end of the lake, drifting about twenty-five yards from shore. It appeared to be empty. A high resonant humming floated across the water, a seemingly aimless ballad, coming and going, sourceless, evanescent. He listened awestruck. Alice's feet appeared over the gunnels, a surreal apparition.

Without any memory of his undressing, he was standing naked beside his neatly folded clothes. Still her song came. He stepped off the embankment. Cold muck sprung between his toes. He eased toward the skiff in quiet breaststrokes. The water became warm, then went icy again. Her humming ceased. The stern swung to meet him. Slowly he eased his head up, propelling himself with his legs so as not to disturb the balance of the skiff.

She lay naked in an inch of tepid bilge, her head on a pair of tennis shoes, ankles resting on the gunnels, one hand draped over her breast, the other between her legs. Though her posture had no apparent intent to arouse, its very casualness fixed his gaze. The air was utterly quiet: only the faint whisper of her hand below her belly and the soft thunk of water against the hull. Sweat stung his eyes. He blinked.

"You like what you see?" Her voice came easefully, without premeditation. He dropped back into the water, surprised, sputtering, then pulled himself up. She lay as before, with a slight smirk, sprawled in an obscenely suggestive posture.

"Damn you," he said.

She laughed. "I could hear you coming, grasshopper."

"Damn you," he repeated in impotent rage.

"Damn you too," she said, and for the first time turned to face him. "Damn you too," she repeated with genuine fury. Then in one swift and almost imperceptible movement, in that lightning sleight of hand she seemed so capable of, she raised an oar and swiped it past his head, its weight carrying her clumsily around. The blade smacked the water. She loosed a stream of abuse, and when he laughed at her rage, which seemed so innocent vested in such naked slenderness, she speared the oar at his face. It skimmed his shoulder, plunged, then shot up, propelling away. While he retrieved it, she mounted the other oar and began to pull, the skiff swirling in futile circles, while she admonished in shrill tirade. As he approached she flailed at him with the remaining oar until it flew from her grasp.

"Go away," she said.

He pushed the oars into the skiff, then, having forgotten his own nakedness, clambered in himself.

"Don't!" she screamed.

"We have to leave."

"I'll leave when I'm ready."

"Alice, you're going home."

"Fuck home! Fuck everything!"

He could not fathom it. He was sure it was a trick.

"I don't get it," he said.

"You wouldn't. You really wouldn't," she said bitterly.

"I gave my word. You got to go home. They'll hang me."

"I wish you had some feelings," she said.

"What do you mean?"

"You really don't get it, do you? Well they ought to hang you. You're dumb, you know that. Dumb!" A wisp of smile crossed her face, and she shook her head with juvenile pomp and superiority.

"I love you," she said simply. "I know it's dumb, but I do."

He snickered nervously. "Well just forget it."

There was a quiet filled with the slap of water against the skiff. An acute heat pulsed in his face.

"I like your tattoo," she mentioned, offhand. "I like what it says."

"Thanks," he said. "I got it on a dare."

"I still like it."

"It's nonsense," he said. His throat tightened. He picked up the oars, stroked toward the shore. "Nonsense, you hear me?"

"Yeah," she said.

He picked up his clothes and dressed himself, turning his back to her. She sat in the bow sneering, mocking him with her nakedness. He rowed with quiet intensity. Maybe I ought to, he thought. Maybe it would cure her. The oars slapped the water and slipped, throwing his balance.

Kitty woke, dressed, climbed down from the loft, and noticed they were gone. She ran to the dock and called for him. Her voice echoed. She shrugged, ignoring the rush of terror, then danced back to the cabin feigning gaiety. She doused her face with water from the kitchen pump, then ate what remained of the celebration banquet.

She climbed back to the loft and began to count the money. A bitter smear moved on her mind. God, I'm jealous. No, it's just he's so dumb. A man is supposed to be logical. Well, let the damn fool if he has to. Her hands seemed to grow hot as she divided the packets into two neat piles, then picked up the scattered bills from the mattress. She put a few loose twenties, then a packet of fifties, then several packets amounting to two thousand dollars inside her purse. A minute later she unsnapped the purse, took out the money, looked at it, then put it back again. She quickly repacked the remaining money into the suitcase, dropped it from the loft, and hurried out to the car. The keys were not there. She bent under the dash and fumbled wildly with a confusion of wires. Enraged, she tore at them. Sparks flew. She beat the black shiny steering wheel as if she could beat the insentient machine into life. She began to curse, enraged that she could not leave, yet partly grateful the betrayal had been sabotaged. Even if he had run off with the girl, it was simply a case of weakness; and the girl was always displaying herself, provoking him. She was just as crazy as he was. She hurried back to the cabin, the suitcase banging her leg. "Dumb," she said, uncertain whether she addressed herself or him or both of them. She took up a half-finished pint of whiskey and drank recklessly, gasping with its fire. She went outside, blinked against the onslaught of sun, and again yelled his name. Her voice echoed in emptiness. She collapsed, her body heavy, exhausted, the previous night's pleasure a wispy dream. She sat drinking on the veranda steps. I'm not going to worry, she said. She lay back, feeling the sun bite her face, and unbuttoned her blouse. The day eased along her skin. Maybe I'm wrong about him, she said in lazy stupor. She allowed herself to recall the wild flutterings that had moved through her belly the previous night, a night that seemed ages ago. But maybe he had nothing to do with it. He means well, but he's not right for me. He thinks I love him. All I want to do is dance.

Again she felt on the verge of tears. She spotted the skiff, and made out the white splashing where the oar blades banged the water. She screamed his name. His voice carried back to her. Thank god, she said.

When he turned the ignition key and the engine did not budge, her face began to burn and she looked away. He swore and turned the key again. He got out and fussed under the hood, cursing: jesus jesus jesus.

"Hit the lights," he told her.

The lights came on.

"It's not the goddamn battery," and again he whispered jesus jesus.

Alice got out of the car and meandered around the clearing. Harry worked under the hood, then he turned and looked at the girl; she stopped moving and he rushed her, grabbing her arm: "All right you goddamn bitch, what'd you do to it?"

The girl stood unblinking in his shower of spittle: "Nothing," she said coolly.

"Goddamn it, tell me or I'll break it." He twisted her arm behind her back. "I swear I will."

"I told you," she said. She tried to pull away. He struck her face. She made no sound, not even a yelp of surprise.

"Leave her alone," Kitty intoned.

"Goddamn it," Harry said, still addressing the girl: "Tell me or I'll break it."

"Don't, grasshopper," she said softly. Her eyes grew bright, glistened.

Kitty yelled to him: "Harry, I think I found it."

He released the girl and returned to the car. He peered

[ *138* ]

under the dash, his breath short and harsh.

"Goddamn it, she messed up the wires. She was trying to wire it."

He began to work, stretched awkwardly on his back, all the while cursing: his life had become a perpetual curse. He tried to calm himself: Soon I can stop running. He tried the key again. This time the engine turned, but would not catch.

"Goddamn bitch!" he yelled out to Alice. "Get your ass over here."

She stood unmoving, a fragile yet somehow invincible statue illumined by a stream of sunlight.

"Why'd you have to try it? Why?"

Her stillness infuriated him. He ran at her. He stopped just short of her and drew his arm back. She refused to flinch.

"Bitch," he said.

"I didn't do it, grasshopper," she said evenly.

Her eyes met his; then he knew what he did not want to know: she was telling the truth. In abject fury he struck her. She fell, not so much from the force of the blow as from a profound disappointment.

"I told you to get in that goddamn car."

"I feel sorry for you," she said, her voice husky.

He knelt in remorse and touched her face. She brushed his hand away.

"I'm sorry," he said. "I told you to get in the car."

"I didn't mess with those wires."

"I know," he said.

Kitty called out: "Come on, we got to get this fixed."

For a moment he stood and stared at her. She sat with a defensive scowl, clutching a cigarette.

It took another ten minutes to get the car started. He was sweating by that time, his whole body shaking with frustration. Alice remained sitting where she had fallen, dropping pine needles over her feet.

"Come on," Harry yelled.

"Just go," Kitty said.

"We can't leave her."

[ 139 ]

"Why not?"

"We got to get her home and get the heat off."

"You shouldn't have hit her."

When he looked at her, Kitty realized what he was thinking.

"I didn't hurt her," he said.

"But it was dumb."

"All right, it was dumb, but if you hadn't—"

He stopped short, not out of fear of falsely accusing, but because he did not want to admit the implications of her attempted betrayal; it would shatter the dream, the dream he lived and risked himself for.

"If I hadn't what?" she said.

"Nothing."

"What do you mean nothing? You think I did it, is that it?"

"I didn't say that."

"But it's what you're thinking. Admit it, Harry."

"No."

"So what if I did?"

"Don't," he said.

"You were off with her doing god knows what. How am I supposed to know what's going through your head?" She was close to screaming.

"She ran off. I just went to get her."

"Oh tell me another one!"

"Forget it," he said.

"I really don't give a fuck who you screw, you hear?"

Once more he started to defend himself, but something short-circuited his breath. He jammed the car in gear and took off with lurching acceleration, mowing down the underbrush. Fifty yards up the road he skidded to a stop, put the car in reverse, and careered backward to the clearing, stopping just short of Alice who still sat in unperturbed meditation.

"You drive," he told Kitty.

He got out and pointed the pistol at the girl's head; his hand began to shake.

"Come on," he said.

Alice did not move.

"Come on, Alice. I can't play games. I'm in too much trouble."

She scooped up a handful of dry humus and slowly showered it over the pistol.

"Leave her," Kitty called. "Tell the cops and let them find her."

"You hear that?" Harry said. His voice shook. "You want it that way? Tell the cops to come out here and get you?"

Without speaking Alice got up, brushed aside the gun, and calmly got in the back seat where she sat, hands primly folded in her lap. They drove out through the hushed sun-struck woods. When they reached the road Harry pointed east.

"I thought we were going to San Francisco," Kitty said.

"East," he said. "I promised to get the bird."

"You got to be kidding," she said.

"I promised."

"Well go ahead," she said and got out of the car, slamming the door. "And I want my cut now."

"Don't be silly."

"Harry, if you're going after that damn bird—"

"I just thought—"

"You're crazy. Insane."

"All right," he said. He was close to tears. For a moment she stood, indecisive, feeling his emotion well up in her. She fought back her own sentiment.

"Jesus, Harry, that bird, I mean—"

"I said forget it, for christ's sake."

"All right."

Kitty got back in and the big white car eased onto the blacktop heading west. After a few minutes Alice spoke in a soft remote tone: "It's too bad about the bird."

Route 26. The blacktop chipped, center strip faded. They had been driving west for five hours, taking turns at the wheel. He had forgot the forces mounting against them. He drove oblivious, serene, with a dreamy notion of a perfect haven ahead. First San Francisco, then a bus east, or north perhaps: yes, a bus because they would be checking the airports, and then . . . then my time is my own . . . then I can be me, he thought.

The road set him at ease: the sudden curve, no diesel stench, just fresh piny wind; this road was a surprise, a tune. He played it, driving one-handed. He held up the pint to the sun, light splitting in the startling amber that would burn in his belly and put the carefree haze in his head. On the straight stretches he closed his eyes, felt the road tremble in his fingertips. He was empty now even of the dreamlike terror that had pursued him for a week. Even his mourning for his bird was sadly sweet.

He looked at Kitty and he could not help himself: he pulled her to him, kissed her wildly for a few seconds until he felt the car drift. She smiled. He was certain she had forgiven him, perhaps even desired him again. He could not dare to believe otherwise. As they were nearing the town of Twain Harte, he was struck by a single illuminated thought: I'm happy. I, Harry Keller, am happy.

Again he pulled her to him and kissed her, and despite

her will not to, she responded. The wind blew against her face, the sun beat against her closed eyes. Even though there was no reason, in fact every reason against it, she felt good. Then came a thought she did not understand: Is this all there is to it? The car swerved and he drew his face away. Instead of reprimand on her tongue, there was laughter, and she thought: I must be going crazy.

The afternoon light had taken on a long cool slant, cutting into their eyes as they descended the western slope of the Sierra and headed toward the coast, and with the waning light there seemed to fall over them a heavy brooding, a tightening of nerves, the exhaustion of magic.

At a little after six they pulled into a town tucked in the sullen shadow of a narrow valley and stopped in front of an antiquated three-story log structure bearing a carved wooden sign: SILVER LODE HOTEL. Half a dozen people sat lounging on the veranda in a wash of dance music emanating from the hotel's interior. They watched with feigned indifference as Harry entered the lobby, where he questioned the desk clerk who proved to be the Greyhound ticket agent. He carefully laid two twenties on the counter and asked for a one-way to Los Angeles.

"The local comes through at seven forty. There's an hour layover in Stockton. Get into L.A. about six A.M.," the clerk intoned.

"Thanks," Harry said and picked up his change.

"Haven't seen you around here," the clerk said.

"No. Just passing through."

"Come and stay sometime," the clerk said.

Kitty sat with a cigarette in her mouth, hiding behind her hand. Alice was perched on the back seat picking at her toenails. When Harry handed her the ticket she let it fall. He cursed once, softly, then went to the trunk and took out her bag, feeling the intent eyes of the hotel loungers. He dropped the bag on the sidewalk.

[ *143* ]

"Come on," he said.

Alice peeled a layer of silver off her toenail and studied it. He snatched her wrist.

"Now," he said. "Out." His grip tightened, burning her skin; he began to pull her forcibly from the car. She let her body drag. The veranda watchers perked.

"Why?" he said.

"I just don't want to."

"Why not?"

She jerked her arm away. "I want a cut."

"Damn it," Kitty said. "They're all listening."

"What kind of cut," Harry said.

"Ten percent."

"For christ's sake, Harry. Let's get out of here," Kitty said.

"Or I don't go home," Alice said.

He tossed her bag into the back seat. Kitty had already taken the wheel and the car was moving when he hopped in. She ran the one stoplight in the middle of town.

"Slow down."

"I can't believe this," Kitty said.

"You better slow down."

On the outskirts of town the road veered north, wending up a steep incline out of the valley.

"Pull over," he said. "Next chance."

"Are you telling me you're going to give her seven thousand dollars?"

"What do you suggest?"

"I suggest we dump her. Right here."

"You hear that, Alice?"

The girl smiled. "Do what you want."

"Pull over, right there," he said.

"Harry, you're not—"

"Shut up. Just shut it up."

She jerked on the handbrake. He slammed the door and stalked away between a cluster of weathered picnic tables and overflowing trash barrels. They were only a few miles from town, but the landscape felt remote and wild. She watched him disappear down a path that dipped toward the lonely rushing sound that permeated the gloomy light. She called to him, but there was no answer except the sibilant rushing. She yelled her threat to leave, knowing he did not hear. She released the brake and the car drifted forward, snapping dry sticks and cedar cones.

"I'm getting out," Alice said.

"The hell," Kitty replied.

"If you're leaving, I'm getting out."

"Go ahead," Kitty said and again set the brakes. "You deserve each other. You really do. You're both insane."

"I guess so," Alice said. "At least we admit it."

"Are you insinuating—"

"I wouldn't think of insinuating anything. Wouldn't waste my time."

"Why you little twat!"

"Little what?"

They faced each other across the seat, the spat exhausted; the intense gloom of the place closed in and a flash of tenderness entered their contempt.

"Why are we talking this way?" Alice whispered.

"You're right."

"Maybe I should get him?"

"No, I'll do it."

As Kitty started down the path, Alice called to her: "Too bad we couldn't be friends." Kitty stopped; her mouth moved, though no words came forth. She hurried on, breaking into a run.

"After all, if it wasn't for me . . ." Alice yelled; but there was no one listening except the brooding woods and empty road.

Harry stood facing the rushing flow, shoulders heaving uncontrollably. salty streams trickling into the corners of his mouth. He felt an impulse to throw himself into the rapids.

It was strange how the sound enveloped him, and how easily he let his tears go, even though they were shameful: it's weakness in a man to cry. Yet he had wanted to, so many times, holding it in. Holding everything in.

"Harry."

He whirled, startled.

"What are you doing?"

"Thinking," he said.

"Don't be mad."

"No," he said.

She approached. "Harry, we got to decide what to do. . . . I want to go home, Harry." There was a quiver in her voice. "You have to make her leave," she said. He nodded. "I mean it."

"I will—she'll go if I give her . . ."

"Are you really going to—"

"It's the only way. She won't turn against us."

He tried to kiss her. Kitty snickered.

"That's all you think about," she said.

"Let's go." A few yards down the path he pulled her to him. "Did you care last night?" he asked.

She shrugged.

"But you liked it. I know you did. I could feel it."

"I don't know. Please, I can't think right now." She pushed her face tenderly against his. "Please," she whispered. "Maybe I did. I'm just so tired."

They returned and took the suitcases from the trunk and went back down the path to a small clearing near the stream. Harry knelt over the packets of money, counting in the hushed solemn atmosphere. Kitty stood watching, her perpetual cigarette smoldering, the smoke rising luminous in the darkening air. When he had finished counting out Kitty's half, she knelt and stuffed the bills into her own suitcase, discarding several pieces of clothing to make room. Then she tossed a packet back.

"My share of expenses," she said.

He did not count the remaining share of money, but simply took out seven thousand dollars and stacked it before Alice's bare feet. There was a long silence filled with the rush of water and a soughing gust through the trees. Alice toppled the stack of bills with her toes, then lackadaisically tossed them into her yellow canvas purse. On the way back to the car, Alice took his arm and stopped him.

"Grasshopper," she said, her voice hushed, her breath beating softly against his face. "I'll go—but you got to promise me."

"What?"

"You got to promise when it all blows over."

"What is it?"

"Send for me."

He started to speak. He could feel her hard determined glare through the darkness; his gaze drifted past her shoulder through the black apparitions of evergreens to the glimmer of rapids.

"Sure," he said.

"Promise?"

"Sure."

"All right," she said. "Then I'll go."

As he drove away he watched her in the mirror. She squatted on the sidewalk beneath the Greyhound sign, occupying the spot as if she were utterly at home. She did not wave or even acknowledge their departure. He felt something in him reach back to her: to her fragility, to the history they shared. His eyes warmed and he bore down on the accelerator.

They headed west, keeping to the back roads. Questions began to crowd him, and fear seemed to grow out of the air. He longed for a place to rest, even an anonymous rented room. He wanted to bathe in hot water, to linger over a hot meal. But despite the suitcase of printed paper, such commonplace domesticity seemed out of reach.

"I need cigarettes," Kitty said.

He nodded, his scalp prickling. She's going to leave, he thought. First chance she gets. He drained the pint of whiskey, head thrown rakishly back, stretching his tongue to catch the last drops. He chucked the empty bottle: the shattering glass whispered in their wake.

"I thought you were the one didn't like trash thrown around," Kitty said.

"What difference does it make?"

She shrugged. "None to me. I always thought you were pretty high and mighty about it."

He picked up a few remnants of trash from the floor and tossed them out. "See, what the fuck difference does it make?"

"I need cigarettes."

"You told me."

"What are we going to do?" she asked. "I mean—now we have the money."

"Like we said. We go to Frisco. Dump the car. Get on a bus."

"Maybe you better change your name."

"Sure, why not? Something gallant maybe. Something with some class."

Kitty looked at him and he could feel the sneer. "Might not sit too well," she said.

"Fuck you too."

"I'm scared."

"You and your goddamn cigarettes."

"Let's just not talk, all right?"

"Listen, I didn't mean it."

"All right, I forgive you."

"*You* forgive *me*? I like that, Katherine. I really like that."

"Glad to hear it."

When he tried to speak, she again cut him off. She switched on the radio and rocked to the static-filled music, shunning him with her private dance.

"Listen," Kitty said. It was a favorite song of his, one he had heard on his way to the warehouse the day, as he put it, *I got fed up and went crazy.*

The song ended and there was a voice speaking in rapid vacuous intonation meant to convey both objectivity and excitation; the voice was jaded with a hundred thousand crimes, wars, natural disasters; it was no one's voice, but it addressed him directly. His face began to glow hot, his legs went loose, his throat ached.

jesus jesus

[ *149* ]

*. . . the terrorist-kidnapper known as Doctor Cloud
has been identified as Harold A. Keller, a Los Angeles television repairman . . . unidentified female
conspirator . . . an undisclosed ransom delivered
. . . as yet no sign of Alice Fisk . . .*

The words etched into his mind so that hours, even days
later, the innocuous clichés of the news report would stab
unexpectedly into his mind.

"Harry, I'm out of goddamn cigarettes."

"Did you hear that? That bastard told them everything!"

"I want my cigarettes," she said.

"It'll be okay," he said. The wind tore his words away.
Then suddenly the car lurched and slowed, the engine dead.
He took his hand from her and slammed in the clutch. Kitty
sat upright, her face pale. "Oh no, oh no." He jammed the
car into a lower gear. There was an objection of metal, a
screaming disintegration. The car squealed to a stop.

He turned the key. The lights dimmed and the music
died. When he released the key the lights returned, and the
radio. He twisted the key a dozen times, each time with the
same result. He could hear the tick of the cooling engine and
a vast sound of crickets. He got out and opened the hood and
stared at the oily beast that had failed him.

"Now you've done it," she said, her voice wavery.

"Sure," he said. "I've done it. The goddamn engine
seized and I've done it."

"We know that, Harry."

He said nothing. He slowly drew the pistol from his belt
and stared at the dead machine. Quite calmly he kicked at a
door panel, then with rising fury kicked again. He knocked
out a taillight with the pistol butt, then continued stalking
around the car, without any appearance of haste or frenzy,
dealing out little destructive blows. "You're nuts," she
told him.

[ *150* ]

He kicked again and slipped.

"It'll beat you, Harry," she said. "It always does, doesn't it?"

He turned. She screamed and hunched over, hands clamped on her head. He shot once, then again, and again, the reverberations mingling with her screams. The gun was empty, shaking in his hand. There were six bullet holes scattered sporadically over the hood of the car. Then only the crickets, the incredible wash of crickets starting up through the ringing in his ears, mingling with the smell of engine grease and the acridity of hot gun. He spoke in an empty dazed voice to no one: "I guess I'm not cut out for this." He gave a last futile kick at a tire. "Goddamn car," he said.

She rose cautiously, peering over the dash. When he looked at her she flinched.

"Sorry I blew up," he said.

"Jesus," she whispered.

"I'm sorry," he said, flaring.

She snatched the keys and got out and went around to the trunk and took out her suitcase, and without a word started down the road.

"Where are you going?"

There was a hesitation in her gait, then her voice came back. "To get some goddamn cigarettes."

"Wait."

Her steps continued to recede, sharp clicks against the blacktop.

"Kitty, god damn it, you can't do this."

He ran after her and went barking around her, pleading, demanding.

"God damn it, you can't."

"Why not?"

"I love you."

She laughed. He lunged, his teeth hitting hers. The suitcase dropped. She pulled her head away and swore. He caught her hair, drew her face to his. They swayed, locked in struggle—then she suddenly went loose, quivering. He covered her face with a flurry of little kisses. She felt very alone, whispered to by a madman on a road that went nowhere; and while he declared his love, she was thinking: I want to go home. Then she was kissing him, pulling him hard against the swollen softness of her mouth. This happened without her being aware she had reversed herself. She no longer listened to the voice calling *it's insane it's insane*, but clung to him in loneliness, feeling his other arm, still encumbered with the gun, move down her back.

"Let's get the blankets," she said, her voice hoarse, gone with a desperate desire simply to be held. But he felt himself draw away. He was sure he could hear the distant whine of tires.

"Harry, you feel me?"

"Yes," he said.

"Harry, hold me. Please hold me."

She shook in his arms. Light rounded a curve and he pulled her down, rolled with her through wet weeds into a ditch. Through her breathing he could hear the cranky banging of a loose tailpipe. When he looked he saw bright lights, burning white, alien beside the white convertible.

"I'm scared," she whispered.

"It's okay."

"I'm scared I've gone crazy."

"Shhh."

"It's the cops, isn't it?"

"No," he said. "It's okay."

"I want a cigarette," she said. "They're going to catch us. They'll kill us, won't they?"

"Don't be silly."

"Harry, I want to go home."

"Sure," he said. "We'll go home."

"Harry." She let out a giggly whimper. "We did it, didn't we?"

"Sure," he said.

"Why is it so important?" she asked, her voice a little girl's.

"I don't know."

Car doors opened. He heard voices. A dog barked.

"Why don't they go?" she whispered.

"The trunk's open. They'll find it. Wait here," he said.

"Harry, don't. We still have my share."

"It's not the cops."

"They'll leave," she said.

"They're going to find it."

He slipped away from her, and in a low crouching run he moved toward the lights. He realized the pistol was empty and cursed. Then his name was called out. The voice was young, petulant, challenging. It was Alice.

The air was rank with marijuana and dog. Harry sat in the back of the rusty automobile with two mixed shepherds, his feet propped on the suitcases. Alice and Kitty sat in front with the man who introduced himself as Dogman, insisting that was his name and he should be called such. He was tall, slender, of indeterminate age, with dark curling hair that fell midway to his back and that he was constantly sweeping away from his eyes. He had a full beard, untrimmed. He talked incessantly, and when he was not talking he was laughing. He drove at extraordinary speeds, yet half the time he was either looking at Alice or letting his gaze drift to Kitty. Harry gritted his teeth as the car swayed on worn shocks, squealing through curves.

"I need cigarettes," Kitty said.

"How'd a joint do you?" Dogman said. He fished in his pocket. "Dynamite stuff," he said. "Just ask Alice. Woooeeeee!"

Alice grinned, vacant, imbecilic.

"Just lucky we happened along," Dogman said. "I been stuck on this hick road for hours without anything goin' by. At night nobody'll stop. Where you folks headed?"

"Frisco," Harry said.

"How about that? You got good karma. Super karma. Headed there myself. Pickin' up some nice stuff. Yep, I spent three days once hitchin' to Frisco from here. Three fuckin'

[ 154 ]

days. Best I ever did it was twenty hours. You can crash tonight at the farm. We leave first thing in the morning."

"I think we'll just move on," Harry said.

"Shit man, I'm tellin' you, there's no way out of here at
night. Unless you got bread for a private limo. The only
thing's going to pick you up is a state trooper or a drunk
redneck wants some pussy. Hell, I'll get you straight to
Frisco. We'll be there tomorrow night easy. Maybe before
dark. Alice here is coming." He laughed, then reached over
and pulled the girl's face to his. The car swerved violently.

"Hey," Harry said. "Let her alone."

The man turned. "Don't get uptight man. We're just
havin' fun." The dog nearest Harry began to snarl.

"It's okay," Alice said.

"Yeah, look what you did, got the dog all upset."

"Sorry," Harry said.

Again the dog snarled.

"Hey Casper," the man said addressing the dog. "The
man said he was sorry. Hey light this fuckin' joint." He
handed it to Alice.

Harry only pretended to smoke. I have to keep clear, he
thought. There was no trusting Alice now. She might blurt
out anything. He would have to make her call again. Maybe
he would call the authorities and tell them where to pick
her up.

The man was talking. Babbling. Harry hitched his jacket
tighter. Under his shirt the heavy weight of the pistol prodded his belly. Suddenly he was spent; he knew he could decide nothing without sleep. If the man had said he was
turning them in, Harry's reaction would have been a weak
exhausted laugh. He dozed, woke, dozed again. The dogs
settled, one of them resting its head in his lap.

He jerked awake when the car stopped. They were
parked beside a country tavern, a couple of gas pumps in
front and a trio of weathered cabins in the rear. A jukebox
was banging out familiar plaints of love. Dogman leapt out

of the car and bawled with flushed joviality: "Here we got your cigarettes, your booze, your greasy burgers, your local color all under the lordship of your friendly neighborhood tavern keeper. Come and get it, folks!"

Harry slipped the gun to the floor and brought up the rear of the little parade Dogman led in antic dance, twirling and whooping.

Four patrons sat in the sullen half-light of the bar: two weathered men who looked as if they had lived in the mountains all their lives, a frowsy blonde about forty, and a quiet younger man who sat alone. Under the proprietor's edgy gaze, Dogman led the way in triumphal pomp, greeting everyone with excessive intimacy. Then without consultation, he ordered four beers.

"I don't want those dogs in here tonight," the proprietor said.

"Now don't get uptight, Mr. Hoosicks."

"I won't, long as they stay out."

"I like dogs," the woman said.

Dogman sidled over and gave her a kiss. "Mildred, you're a sweetie." Dogman lifted her off the barstool and whirled her through a few shrieking waltz steps.

"You people jus' don't 'preciate things," the woman said. "Jus' because he's friendly, ain't no sin."

"Oh jesus, Mildred," the barman said. The young fellow sitting alone smiled and got up to throw darts. Instantly Dogman left the woman to challenge him. The young man handed him the darts and sat back down without a word.

"You folks want these beers?" There were four unopened bottles on the bar.

"Sure," Alice said.

"I'm going to have to see your I.D., little lady."

"It got ripped off," Alice said. "Really it did."

"I'm sorry, little lady," Hoosicks said.

Dogman fired the darts, then came to the bar with his sly wheedling challenge, asking the barman how long they had known each other. Kitty dumped coins into the cigarette dispenser. Harry edged away from Dogman and the proprietor, his glance drifting to the television set above the bar. It needed tuning. Automatically his mind moved through the rituals of adjusting it, like a mechanic fussing his mind over an engine. Then he was not only looking at the screen, but seeing the picture: a photograph of Alice. He looked away. Kitty put four packs on the bar; then her fingers dug into his arm.

"Jesus, Harry," she whispered.

"Don't look. Go feed that jukebox."

"I'm out of change. Oh god—"

"Don't look, damn it!"

He meandered with stilted nonchalance to the jukebox, an ancient glowing Wurlitzer with a window to observe the records being selected and played. He dropped a coin and pretended to be looking over the selections, but his eyes of their own moved back to the screen. He was traveling in eerie slow motion through the apartment at Casa Désirée. A hand pointed to the unfolded sofa bed and the camera closed in with obscene interest on the wrinkled sheets, as if probing for telltale remnants. A queasy thrill ran through him when the camera panned suddenly across a somber hardfaced man, a detective perhaps, and moved into the kitchen, over the coffee cups they had left like artifacts of another life, then on to the saucer of cigarette stubs; a hand picked one up and held it to the camera. The next instant they were in the bedroom amidst the luxuriant growth of marijuana; leaves were touched and pointed to. Then the camera weaved across the pallet where Alice had lain. Next there was a photograph of himself, a duplicate of the identification-card shot issued by Meany's TV, with a verbal description mentioning his tattoo.

The drunk lady got off her stool and came forward, her eyes rapt, focused on the television screen: "Why don'tcha all shuddup? I wanna hear the news. So why don'tcha all—"

"Sit down, Mildred," the barman said.

Harry pressed the jukebox keys; the machine whirred.

"Turn it up," the woman said. "With all this shit goin' on I can't hear nothin'."

A ballad of unrequited love a decade old, worn and scratchy, thumped softly into the room.

"No," Dogman was saying. "This man"—he pointed a hooked finger at Hoosicks—"this man has known me since I was a kid."

"A real blessing," the barman said. "How old are you anyway, little lady?"

Alice shrugged, her face locked in intoxicated grin.

"Wonderful," the barman said.

"Listen, Mr. Hoosicks," Dogman said, "who is ever going to know?"

"Let's just go," Harry said. "Buy some beers and we'll go."

"Now I can't go selling this gentleman beer knowing I'll be contributing to the delinquency of a minor."

Alice giggled. "Boy, if you only knew," she said to no one in particular.

Hoosicks took the beers off the counter. "Out" he said.

"Now just a second," Dogman said.

"I'll wait outside," Harry said. "Come on, Kitty." They started toward the door.

"Now don't be like that," Dogman said. "Have a beer."

"If you want a beer, have one," Harry said. He tossed a bill on the bar.

"You having a beer or not?" Hoosicks said to Dogman.

"Ahh hell, give me a sixpack."

The proprietor hesitated, then put a carton on the bar and made change.

"Come back soon, you sweeties," the woman said as they filed out.

If anything, Dogman's driving now was even more erratic, though he was oblivious to the tension this caused his passengers. He ranted for some time about the barman, stating repeatedly that he would get even. "People ought to be

friendly," he insisted. "They just ought to be. I'm friendly."
He rapped his chest with his fist.

"Maybe he had a rough day," Kitty suggested.

"Rough day? Every day's a rough day," Dogman said.
The car lurched and fishtailed squealing around a curve. Dogman rambled on with absolute confidence, driving now by
pure instinct. At first the errant motions of the car kept
Harry's mind from the broadcast; his eyes strained trying to
pick out the road ahead of the headlights as if he could somehow will the car's course by vision alone. Finally the fear of a
smash-up burrowed so deeply into him, it settled in a cold
futile lump, and he began to relive the television images,
irate at the public invasion of his domicile. After all, they
had his last month's rent. He felt special indignation at the
prying into his bed: as if the wrinkled sheets implied some
evil. And the saucer of cigarette butts. What had they
meant by that? It enraged him that he would have no chance
to make a case for himself—not to justify, he knew there was
no justification. The law was the law. It wasn't supposed
to make exceptions or understand. He accepted this, but he
still wanted someone to understand. He wanted the drunk
woman in the bar to understand, and all the old people in
their tired rooms whose tired lives he'd tried to cheer, who
might remember him: he wanted them to understand. Why
this was so important he could not have said; like a man
trying to explain why he'd given up all comfort and security
to create something he thought was beautiful. All I really
wanted to do was know who I was, Harry thought. And
they're going to make me out something else before I even
find out myself.

The car veered onto a gravel road that rose steeply
through heavy pine, then into wet moonlit pasturage. The
road was heavily rutted, and as the car squirreled he was
thrown against the sleeping dogs, who woke and perked,
smelling home territory. They rumbled across a cattle guard,
then spun up a steep muddy slope and came to a large wood-

frame farmhouse, its roof gleaming silver in the moonlight. The car stopped in a muddy yard halfway between the house and the barn where half a dozen other ramshackle vehicles stood. They were greeted by the baying of a swirling pack of mongrels that leapt, paws scraping at the windows.

"Welcome to Rainbow Ranch," Dogman said. "Finest accommodations for outlaws in the West."

Dogman lurched out into the yard, greeting the dogs by name, laughing under their leaps. His own dogs joined the pack. Harry tucked the pistol in his belt, pulled his jacket over it, and followed with the two suitcases across the muddy yard.

Despite the late hour, the great rambling house was awash with people drinking, smoking, playing musical instruments. Their arrival seemed to generate fresh festivities, as if the occupants of the house were completely aware of their crime, yet welcomed them as criminal heroes. Dogman's introductions were in keeping with this atmosphere, which left both Kitty and Harry in a state of giddy paranoia.

The living room, bulwarked at one end by a mammoth fieldstone fireplace ablaze with four-foot logs, held more than a dozen people who seemed to be in a constant process of interchange with another dozen, so the new arrivals were treated to a phantasmagoria of faces, introductions, and handclasps. Even the babies, two of which crawled naked about the room, were introduced. All this time a young woman, no older than Alice, held a nursing baby to her breast and sang softly in a lush soprano. This woman seemed clean, somehow untouched by the scruffy demeanor of the others. And too young to have brought forth a child. Harry caught himself envisioning the birth: he had once seen a sequence of photographs in a medical book, and they had so impressed him that for weeks the images had haunted him at inappropriate moments until he had thought he was mad.

[ 161 ]

He noticed Kitty watching the young mother too, her face rapt, almost longing. He touched her hand. She responded, her fingers squeezing his, and he felt a rush of well-being swell through him. He longed to tell her it was all going to be okay.

He brought out his harmonica and played a soft accompaniment to the young woman's singing. When the song ended there was applause. He continued to play, and for half an hour he managed to forget himself in the music, wine, and smoke. Then he recalled Dogman's reference to the ranch being an accommodation for outlaws; his mind raced, thinking perhaps they had already been turned in. Then it occurred to him that of course they would not turn them in at all. In panic he stopped playing and moved to the stairwell where he had left their luggage. It was still there. Someone behind him touched his arm and he whirled, his abruptness betraying his fear.

"I really dig your playing," the woman said.

"Thanks," he said.

"I'm Starcrest."

"Yes," he said nodding.

"Your lady is really beautiful," she said. Her voice was soft, close, intimate. She smiled. He smiled back, and picked up the suitcases, thinking, Why is she telling me this?

"Aren't you going to play again?"

"I'm beat."

"Dogman said you're in a hurry to get to San Francisco."

"Yeah, sort of."

"He's going straight there in the morning. You into dealing?"

"Not really," he said.

"Just wondered."

"It's all right."

"It's just the way you're holding onto those, it's like you got a ton of hash in them or something."

For a second he was lost—then through a forced grin he heard himself say: "Boy, I wish."

[ 162 ]

She laughed and her hand brushed his middle, then quickly drew back.

"What's that?"

"A keepsake," he said.

"A gun?" she said, still smiling.

"Say, is there someplace I could park these and lay down?"

She hesitated, then said: "Listen, I'll get your lady." He watched her make her way across the crowded living room. She was a woman of thirty or so, her heavy dark hair streaked with a few strands of early gray. He felt sorry for her, though he didn't know why. Maybe it was her eyes. Or her friendliness that seemed too open. Then he recanted, thinking, I'm too conventional. There are people who just take life as it comes. There are people who trust. Spontaneous people. He felt an acute yearning to be like them. Yet part of him rebelled, sensing something too calculated in this seeming freedom. In a way they were no better off. Still, there was something to be learned. Only there was never enough time.

The woman returned, holding Kitty's hand in hers, their fingers interlaced. Kitty was glassy-eyed, her mouth drawn in a perpetual smile. When her hand touched his, it was icy.

The house seemed to ramble endlessly on, most of its various bedrooms empty. Once they passed a room from which issued unmistakable sounds of love, and he hesitated, thinking it was Alice, trying to find her identity in the rhythmic expulsions of breath. But already Starcrest and Kitty had noticed his hesitation. He moved on. At the end of the hallway Starcrest put her ear to a door, then cautiously opened it.

A piece of faded madras draped on the ceiling softened the overhead light. In one corner lay a double mattress covered with rumpled quilts, beside it a box with candles, a pipe, a paperback book. In another corner a bureau, and on it a small television set. Harry set the suitcases by the bed. There was a moment of silence. Starcrest touched Kitty's hair, then embraced her. Kitty stared ahead, apparently oblivious. Harry touched the woman's shoulder: "I think it's better if we're alone," he said.

"Oh," she said. She cupped her hand briefly to Kitty's cheek. "See you later," she whispered and brushed her mouth with hers. Kitty stood entranced, asleep on her feet.

"Did you see that baby?" she murmured.

"Yes."

"I'm so stoned." And she began to whimper, the relentless whimpers of a small child. He held her, combing his hand through her hair in long strokes.

"It's okay," he whispered.

She clung to him.

"I'm scared."

"It's all right. We just have to be careful not to make anyone uptight."

She nodded and whispered, barely audibly: "I want to go home."

"You are home," he said. "With me."

"I want some water," she sniffled.

He found an unoccupied bathroom and fetched back water in a dirty cracked cup. She gulped it down and asked for more. He refilled it and returned. She was standing at the window.

"You're sweet," she said. He watched her drink with a feeling that somehow her action meant more than the simple drinking of water, but the meaning evaded him.

"I wish I could love you," she said.

"We have the money now," he said. "Think where we can go."

"Funny, isn't it? I mean it's so hard to believe." Kitty collapsed onto the bed. "I'm so tired. I'll be so glad . . ." She yawned again. He covered her, and after putting the gun under the quilts and removing his shoes, he curled next to her, huddling against her back, shivering. Her bottom nestled into his loins. He undid his zipper and pressed against her, but exhausted beyond his desire, his muscles refused to work.

[ *164* ]

The match brought him awake: he saw the woman's face and tried to remember her name. She put her mouth to the pipe. She sat on the edge of the mattress next to Kitty.

"Want some?"

He shook his head and closed his eyes, feeling himself sink back into slumber. The woman's voice was fuzzy, remote. "I thought you'd still be up."

He didn't answer, feigning sleep. The woman smoked awhile; then he heard her undress and felt her slip under the covers next to Kitty. Suddenly he was awake, his heart hammering. The woman's hand moved over his own, inside Kitty's blouse. He heard the woman's breath, little kissing sounds. He lifted his head. The woman's face came toward his.

"I don't think we're really into this," Harry said.

"Shhh."

"We're so beat."

"I like you," she said.

"Yeah, well—"

"Shhhh."

He felt an urge to laugh: this business was simply part of the outlaw's job. The winds blew and you had to adapt. If it meant humoring this woman, so be it.

"I really don't think she's into this," he whispered.

The woman didn't answer. He lay there trying to ignore

[ 165 ]

the woman's hands nestling under Kitty's clothes, and the little sounds she made, trying to ignore them because the sound and movement excited him, and this excitement seemed somehow soiled, not so much because he did not like the woman, but because he had conspired with her out of fear. He was resentful that she was taking advantage, and' guilty that he was allowing it. He tried to consider the woman's affection as genuine, but he was suspicious of any immediate attractions, even his own. He lay with his mind swirling in vexed amazement at his own confusion.

Kitty murmured and he felt her legs open. He wondered if her movement was conscious cooperation, or merely a sleepbound reaction to sensory disturbance. If she woke, would she scream? Would she blame him? The woman moved down under the quilts. He touched Kitty and the woman's hand came over his, took it, and pulled it across her breast. Then she took his hand to her mouth, and he let her have it, as though it were no longer part of him. Her tongue curled his finger, then she pushed his hand across Kitty's belly, and he felt the woman's tongue between his fingers, and now she arranged him so he was holding Kitty open. Kitty thrust against his hand, against the woman's mouth. Then the woman took him and pulled him down.

"Get behind me," she whispered.

His body was moving on its own. He was still telling himself he mustn't, when she pushed her buttocks into his belly, and reaching between her legs pulled him into her. He felt ridiculous perched over her back, so he drew out—but as soon as he had slipped away, he had to return. When he did, the woman moaned. Her head moved with new vigor and he heard soft kissing sounds, her womb contracting with sharp excitement he sensed derived not from him but Kitty. Kitty's head began to turn, mouth parted, her face drawn in a mask of excitation. And by her sounds she liked it, more than liked it, and for some reason it thrilled him to see her so roused by the ministrations of this woman. Suddenly he came, short quick jabs, exquisite almost to the point of pain. And as if she had felt his coming through the other woman, Kitty started, then bolted upright. Her voice was sharp, cold, trembling. "What are you trying to do?"

"Take it easy," the woman said.

"Harry, what the fuck's happening?"

"It's okay," the woman said.

"Harry, get me out of here," Kitty said. The woman touched her face. "Don't," Kitty said, thrusting the woman's hand away.

"Are you all right?" the woman asked.

"Tell her to leave me alone."

He stammered something, his voice broken, unconvincing. There was strained silence. Harry could see fear and fury work on Kitty's face. He touched her, and she cringed.

"It's just this is where I usually sleep," the woman said.

"I'm sorry," Harry whispered.

"You should've told me," the woman said.

"I did," he said.

"No, you didn't. But no hard feelings, okay?" Again she tried to touch Kitty's face. "I really love you," she whispered.

"Don't," Kitty said.

"Listen, I don't feel right about this," Harry said. "Maybe there's someplace else—"

"No," the woman said. "It's okay." She got up and moved toward the door. "You're sweet," she said. He listened to her feet move down the hall.

He lay next to Kitty, a wealth of unspoken thoughts rising up in him. His penis was cold, shriveled with guilt. Kitty's back was a vibrating barrier he dared not touch. He curled an inch from her, within the aura of her warmth, listening. The house breathed with tiny noises he could not identify. He had too much imagination; it was the imagination of fear and longing. Suddenly he thought of the pistol and reached for it, searching. He got on hands and knees, moving around the bed.

"Go to sleep," she said.

"The gun," he said. "I can't find it."

Indifferent with fatigue, she whispered a curse, then joined the search.

"You sure you had it?"

He was not sure. He had a memory of having it, of placing it under the covers, but he had no idea if the memory was real or imagined.

"Don't leave me," he said and the words felt as if they had been said before, the moment repeating itself from a dream.

"Here," she said and held up the pistol with an expression of disdain.

"It'll be okay," he said. "Everything will be okay."

"Sure," she said. "Sure."

Don't leave me, he thought, still experiencing an uncanny sense of life repeating itself.

Once again he lay beside her. When he finally touched her, she eased away from him. His heart fell; it was the end of the world. He could feel their separation as if it had already happened.

The dawn had already grayed when he fell asleep, his body exhausted by turbid thought. He had planned to stay awake to guard the suitcases, even though their contents had become abstract, almost beyond his interest. Yet this money had to be guarded, whether out of habit, or a sense of duty, or because he had no other purpose, he did not know. Finally his body refused to understand any purpose but its own need for rest, and it pulled his mind into fathomless dreamless sleep. Two hours later, he shot up. Sunlight streamed in the window. Cocks crowed. The sounds of human bustle filtered from below.

He left Kitty asleep, and cautiously went downstairs. Once again the faces passed before him, their greetings fraught with hidden intentions under excessive cheer. He remembered the gun upstairs. All the time he was smiling and greeting the vaguely familiar faces swirling around the stove where coffee flowed from an immense blackened percolator. He wanted them to leave him alone, though at the same time he clung to the distraction of their presence. Then for a moment his paranoia lifted and he felt he could live there, grasping each day as it came, sharing bed and work without ambition or thought of the future, connected only to the cycles of nature, a part of something spontaneous, free, like the woman, Starcrest, who had come to them simply wanting to share.

In a surge of buoyant feeling, he walked out into the yard. Dew steamed out of the grass. In a pasture below the barn a group of children scampered from a goat. A pair of tracks meandered down a slope to a small pond where a rowboat moved over the glassy surface. A woman came from the barn bearing eggs in her lifted apron. He recognized her as Starcrest and quickly turned and walked around the house. There, in a huge oak, its leaves sunstruck and luminous, Alice swung in a tire hung by a rope. A child of five or six pushed her, while a trio of young boys tossed acorns at her from a platform in the tree. She laughed, fending off the missiles, spinning the tire as she swung. She waved. He waved back, confused by her serenity. She let go of the swing and sailed. He would always remember that moment of flight. She seemed magically suspended. When she landed she tripped on a root and rolled lightly and easefully, as if this fall were deliberate. She smiled and extended her hand. He pulled her up. She embraced him, thrusting her tongue between his teeth.

"Bad boy," she said smirking.

"What did you tell him?"

"Tell who?"

"Dogman."

"Him," she said with facile disgust. "What a crackpot."

"What's he know?"

"Oh grasshopper, you do make a mess of things," she said, suddenly serious.

"Alice," he said.

"It's such a beautiful day," she said and her voice quavered.

"Alice, this isn't some diddly little game."

"I know," she said. "But—" Her voice broke.

"Does he know anything?"

"You think I'd do that?" she said with a burst of anger. "You think I'd blow it for us like that?" Her eyes were glassy. "You don't understand anything."

[ 170 ]

"You're right," he said.

"I feel sorry for you, grasshopper."

"I think you've said that."

"And why do you think I slept with that creep last night? Because I wanted to?"

He stood in numb shock, his throat tight, choking off speech. Her fist hammered his chest.

"For *you*, dummy! So he'd do what I wanted! So he wouldn't turn you in!"

"I'm not taking that," he said.

"You don't have to," she said shrugging. "Really, sometimes you're such a creep yourself."

The children called to her.

"You've got to go home, Alice. You've got to stop dreaming."

"Me dreaming?" she sneered.

"Don't cross me," he said.

"Oh you fool," she said and walked back to the children, picking one of them up and swinging her around; Alice squealed, her narrow hips both immaculate and corrupt, challenging him with her delight.

"Harry, come on." It was Kitty who called from the battered sedan, color of clay and rust, the car eroding into the earth before it had even stopped running, Harry thought. He looked at Alice, standing by the open door. The way she was smiling she had to be stoned. All these people going through life stoned. He smiled. The sweat trickling under his arms amused him. TV all the time telling you not to sweat. He waved, picked up the two suitcases, and walked toward the sedan clustered by a lolling crowd who might or might not know what he carried. He felt inebriated, as though he had just discovered he was on stage and thousands were applauding simply because he was himself: Harry the Bold, Harry the Reckless, Harry the Gentle, a winner in his own sweepstakes. Yes, maybe he'd continue, become a sort of Robin Hood. His step was jaunty, and he had to quell the urge to whoop: it was a baffling euphoria, sourceless, frightening.

He looked at Alice. "Well this is it," he heard himself say. Then again the faces. Familiar now. Hands gripping his. All the hands he'd touched. Wonderful, so many hands. Women kissed him square on the mouth. Starcrest clung to him, tightly, then kissed him. There were calls, applause, and she stepped back smiling, then she moved toward Kitty, who let Starcrest embrace her but averted her face to avoid the woman's kiss.

[ 172 ]

"Next time," Starcrest said gently.

For a split second, a long instant, Harry thought: I must be dreaming. Then Alice pulled him into the car.

"Whaaahoooooeeeee!" It was Dogman yelling. Tires whipped loose dirt into the air and the car lurched off, thunking through potholes, rising on half-dead springs, thunking again, the dogs yipping at the wheels.

"Goodbye goats," Harry said to a chorus of waves.

"Jesus, Harry, are you stoned?" Kitty said.

He gazed at her face and was overwhelmed by desire.

"What's the matter?" she asked, looking away. He could still hear the dogs cutting through the woods, snaking along shortcuts, hoping the car would stop. For a moment he was out there with them: running. Nothing particularly mattered. . . .

Her hand was against his chest, keeping him from kissing her. Her face moved, liquid. So many different faces. Colors rose and fell in the shadows. Maybe they put something in the wine. Or maybe it's me. Just me. Going insane. He burst into laughter.

"Right on," Dogman said.

Alice turned and leaned her chin on the seat. Soft brown eyes. Kiss.

"Harry?"

He shook his head, still laughing.

"He's stoned out of his fuckin' gourd," Dogman said, and he laughed too. The car swerved.

"The wine," Dogman said.

Suddenly Harry slapped his face. The gun. Under her mattress.

"Stop," he said.

"What?"

"No," he said. "It's all right. Maybe it's better."

"What?" Kitty whispered. He pushed his face through her curls, felt his lips touch her ear. "The gun. I left it." He smiled and shrugged. The car moved onto asphalt and Harry watched the dogs give up, moving in restless circles on the cracked blacktop.

The sun held. A pipe was passed, relit, passed again. A half-gallon of cheap rosé moved from mouth to mouth. Harry did not realize they had been on the road for less than an hour; it seemed to him days. Every signpost, tree, every turn in the road reverberated with significance; yet he knew it was a carnival ride: he would come down to the land of worry and paranoia.

They crossed a bridge a car-length long. The car slowed, then stopped, tilting at a rakish angle on a grassy shoulder.

"Here it is," Dogman whooped.

"What?"

"My little farm. About a mile upstream. Dogman's vacation. I gotta get some samples and cut 'em back."

"Great," Kitty said with broad sarcasm. "So what are we supposed to do?"

"Have a picnic, have a swim, frolic, rollick, stay high, sigh—"

"I'd throw in a hundred to forget this stop," Harry said.

"Man, you're in too big of a rush. It's no way to go through life. No way."

"He's right," Kitty said. "Remember, you said yourself we gotta keep cool."

"Right on," Dogman said.

Harry counted out five twenties. Dogman grinned. "Shit, I really didn't think you had it."

"Cold cash."

"And plenty more where that came from, I bet," Dogman snickered.

"Sure," Harry said, "I'm loaded."

"Yeah, I got my cash crop coming in soon too—woooeee!" He tipped the jug, gulping; beads of wine caught in his beard.

"So what d'you say we take off?"

"Ahh man, I got to check my crop. I just got to."

"Two hundred," Harry said.

"Don't tempt me, man. You'll be there by supper. Listen, I can't take your money. It wouldn't be fair."

Dogman lurched out of the car with the jug still in hand and grabbed Alice, his body arching over hers. She struggled out of his arms, shaking her finger in mock admonition. Dogman lunged, heavy, drunken, laughing, and as the girl dodged, he fell rolling, the half-gallon jug held upright, unspilled. In an instant, as if this pratfall had been a mere whimsy of courtship, he was on his feet lumbering after her. Alice screamed and ran down an embankment toward the river.

"He's out of his mind," Kitty said.

"Yeah, just a bit."

"Well, are you just going to let him rape her?"

Kitty got out and slammed the door.

"He's not raping her, for christ's sake."

She continued to move away, descending the embankment. He followed, reading the anger in her back. When he caught up, she stopped and turned, her face bright.

"You're right," she said.

"Right?" He was puzzled.

"I was only worried you'd get blamed if anything happened."

"Happened?"

"With Alice and that guy."

"That's her business," he said sullenly. "I thought he knew something. Now I'm not sure."

"We're just paranoid," she said.

He nodded. "We've got to be cool."

"You're right, absolutely right." She kissed him, hard, clinging, pushing her body into his.

"We got to stop acting like goddamn criminals," she panted, then kissed him again. "I mean," she said, "we didn't hurt anyone."

[ 175 ]

"No," he said.

"We're just doing what they always told us," she said. "Looking after ourselves."

She turned a pirouette, inexplicably gay, opening her arms to the sun. Harry smiled, his head wheeling with resurrected euphoria. He watched her dance down a path toward the river. A happy nymph. He started to accompany her on the harmonica.

Dogman and Alice emerged in a flurry of movement, he stumbling, she teasing him with her agility. He still carried the sloshing jug.

"Hey," Harry said.

Dogman stopped, swayed. "Hey," he called back.

"Where's this famous spot of yours?"

Dogman hooked his arm into the air, and they followed him along a rudimentary path for a quarter-mile to where the path opened into a grassy flower-strewn glade that overlooked a pool in the river. The water fell over series of rock terraces to the pool, where shadows of trout hovered in the green depths. A huge cedar spanned outward over the sunstruck water. There was a primeval hush, a rather solemn gaiety about the place that quieted even Dogman.

Harry was sent back for the forgotten knapsack of provisions. He was no more than fifty yards from the glade when he stopped. The shadows switched and played. The rush of the river grew remote. He could hear the ancient drone of growth. The moving woods were littered with birdsong. He moved on. He was lost. He stopped again. Then just as he was about to call out he caught a glint from the car.

The trip back was faster. Though he was certain he had been gone over an hour, it had been no more than fifteen minutes when he broke back into the glade to see Alice dive naked into the pool. Dogman dived after her. Kitty lay in the sun, still clothed; he felt a pang of sadness, sharp, ineffable, that had something to do with her still being dressed; yet had he returned to find her naked, he realized, he might have felt exactly the same way.

"Hey, why don't you folks come in?" Dogman called up from the pool.

"Later," Harry said.

"What's wrong with you people?"

"Guess we don't know how to live," Harry said.

"You act proud of it," Dogman yelled.

"That's right," Harry said.

"Harry—don't!" Kitty whispered.

"I'm getting fed up," he said.

"He's just stoned."

"That's what I said last night when that woman—"

"That's different," she said.

"What's so different?"

"Damn it, Harry—"

"Why don't we take off our clothes then?"

"I don't feel like displaying myself."

"What about dancing at the club?"

"You think I liked that? You really think—" She shook her head in disgust.

"Hey." It was Dogman clambering up the bank. "I didn't mean to get anyone uptight."

"I guess it just comes natural," Harry said.

Dogman laughed and picked up the jug. He drank in great noisy gulps, his belly muscles heaving. His body glistened, tanned and hard. Harry saw Kitty trying not to look. His body was loose, alive, animal, handsome to a woman, Harry thought. Alice emerged after him. They were both long, sinewy, with nothing of excess. They would look good together, he thought.

Dogman offered the jug. Harry shook his head. He offered it to Kitty, his eyes fixing on her, challenging. She took it and drank. He squatted next to her, his nakedness casual, insinuating. He was so at ease. Drunk. Just drunk is all. I could be like that drunk enough.

"I'm starving," Alice said, and knelt, shivering, teeth chattering. She took the wine and drank, then made a grimace. "Don't let me drink any more."

Dogman laughed. "A lady who knows her limits." He draped his arm on her shoulder, pulling her toward him. She squirmed away.

"Little tiger," Dogman said, still laughing.

"I think I've had about my limit on you," Alice said.

"You just think you do, little tiger," Dogman said.

"I know what I think."

Dogman pawed the air and snarled. "So, you dig Harry here?"

"Maybe," Alice said.

"Let's eat," Harry suggested.

"Just a minute, man," Dogman interjected. "I'm askin' this little honeypie a question."

"Leave her alone," Harry said.

"Oh yeah?" Dogman said.

"Yeah," Harry said.

"She your old lady too?"

"Everybody cool it," Alice commanded. There was a silence. Then Dogman said: "All I want to do is get high, and this little chickie has been leadin' me on all day, that's all. So call her off."

"I'm just sick of sex is all," Alice said.

"Amen," Kitty said.

"Okay," Dogman said shrugging. "No big deal. Pass me that sandwich."

They ate in silence. The silence of sun on skin. The silence of insect-thrumming, of water threshing stone.

"Harry." It was Kitty; she took the smoke from him, pursed her lips, closed her eyes. Everybody wants to get high, even the ones saying they can live without it. Can live without a lot of things, but is it worth it? Afraid to get high because you got to come down. Like us, not taking off our clothes. Wishing. He looked at Alice. He imagined the slender boy's body spread, legs raised, himself between, thrusting.

"Harry," Alice said and pushed the rolled paper into his

[ 178 ]

fingers. He couldn't stop grinning. How can they talk? Want to fuck her. Fuck them both. Mouth all dry, wanting. He rolled over and pushed his nose into the grass, feeling his hardness against the earth. Could fuck the earth. Make a hole and put it in. The sun, rain, magic in it. Why can't I stay this way?

"Look at that mother," Dogman laughed. "Stoned out of his skull."

Harry's mouth moved. He tried to speak: he was laughing. Kitty bent over him, giggling.

"Go ahead, man." He felt a hand push him toward the girl.

"Kiss her."

He heard Kitty squeal, saw her scramble to her feet. "Don't you dare touch me." She pointed at Dogman, who, on hands and knees, panted in mimicry of a dog. Harry struggled to his feet, grasped a moment of sobriety.

"Why don't we check your crop?" he said.

Dogman smiled: "Yeah. Yeah, good idea."

"Let's go," Harry said.

Dogman rambled into his clothes, legs thrashing, missing, striking again. Kitty giggled in antic hilarity. Alice sat grinning at private visions. When Dogman finished dressing, he whooped around, charged into the woods, then charged back, shooting his fingers at them like pistols. "Be right back," he said. "Wait right here." He looked at his wrist where no watch was and laughed. "I'll bring back some good stuff."

"Okay," Harry said.

"One hour," he stated again. He spoke like one unfamiliar with the language, grinning at each word, nodding.

"I take Alice," he said.

Harry shook his head. "Alice is in no shape."

"No shape," Alice mocked, sprawled to the sun.

"Need to fuckee," Dogman said, straddling her slender body.

[ *179* ]

"Fuckee when you come back," Harry said. "Business before pleasure."

"Right," Dogman said, saluting. Harry saluted back. Dogman took off crashing into the woods, moving upriver. Harry blinked against the bright blue wash of sky. High as a kite. But I can't let go. Not yet. Wonder what he's thinking? Probably thinks his daughter is in some ditch, poor bastard. Wish he could see her. If I have to tell it in court, they won't believe. He heard himself laughing.

"What?" Kitty said.

Harry geared up his mouth to speak: it was full of fur.

"What's so funny, Harry?"

He shook his head, speechless.

"Poor boy is cracking up," Alice said.

"Afraid so," Kitty concurred.

Conspiracy. Females. Bitterness: all the wrong she feels men did. He stopped laughing. His belly ached. He tore off his shirt and made a noise at the sun. His hands at his belt, then the air brushing his legs. He raised his arms, looked down and saw his penis lift, stand straight, absurd hardness of blood risen for pleasure. He watched his hand go around it; fingers close; squeeze, lift.

"For god's sake, Harry," Kitty said.

But he did not stop. Even the grin would not stop. Silly boy. Alice shook her head in mock pity.

"Poor boy. All lonely."

He stroked himself again, counting. On the verge, so hot. Then he turned away and ran, feet tender. He skittered out on the cedar, teetering over the green pool. He spun, midair, hit the water. Watched the bubbles going up. Then the cold reached him. He burst into the air and his arms strove for shore.

He dived several more times while they watched. The third time he came up Alice was not there. Kitty grabbed his arm and told him to dress.

"She went to pee," she whispered. "Now's our chance."

"But—"

"Christ, Harry, are you that far gone?"

He shrugged: the habitual gesture. All my life shrugging.

"The keys," he said. "I forgot to get the goddamn keys."

"Wire it," she said.

"We can't just dump her."

"Harry, if you don't—"

"Okay. Okay."

She ran ahead urging him on. The woods seemed suddenly immense and their friendliness turned dark and brooding. A mosquito landed on his wrist. He watched it drink, then before it could take off, he slowly crushed it, spreading a smear of blood. Sweat streamed off his body. He had to lie down. Anywhere. He did not care about mosquitoes, the root-ridden earth. It would soon rain. Cooling, cleansing rain.

A scream burst at him: it took the shape of his name. His chest sparked with a jolt of soberness.

"Harry!"

She came running.

"It's gone!"

"What?"

"It's gone! You fool, it's gone!" She shook him, screaming, then collapsed, falling slowly down his body, crumpling at his feet.

"What?"

"The car. The bastard tricked us." Her fist pounded weakly against the ground, then she lay limp.

He shook his head, grinning, imbecilic: "What?"

"Dogman stole the car," she sobbed.

He was running. He stumbled; bare roots tore his outflung hands. He rose bleeding, not caring. When he broke onto the road he froze, closed his eyes, counted softly to himself, then looked again. He ran to where the car had been and fell to his knees.

"Bastard," he whispered without emphasis. "Goddamn dirty bastard. He knew. He knew all along."

Kitty was sitting where he had left her, staring vacantly toward the river.

"We'll get it back," he said.

She snickered listlessly. He sat beside her; but when he tried to hold her she shrugged away. He picked a stem of grass and chewed its sweetness, his jaw working slowly, splitting the fibers. He took a breath and lay back. The earth seemed to move a hand up to hold him. Gone, he thought, and a laugh caught in his throat.

The entire landscape was bathed in eerie green light, the sky black, boiling. Goosebumps prickled his skin. The wind gusted, fell, gusted again. It came in a seething roar, drops hurled with stinging fury. In seconds they were drenched. For a moment they stood transfixed, as if the rain had entered their heads and temporarily drowned despair.

The deluge continued for half an hour in relentless opaque sheets. They took shelter under the bridge, where they had a vantage point of the road. But no car passed. The downpour settled into steady rain, and visibility increased to perhaps a hundred yards. Kitty's teeth began to chatter and he took off his saturated jacket, wrung it, and draped it on her shoulders. He detected a faint change in the wash of sound, then glimpsed a light. The light became two. Harry scrambled to the road and in the distance saw a figure race in front of the lights. The car swerved, then stopped. Even in the gray-green light, Alice's pale towhead seemed to glisten as she stepped into the car. He called Kitty up and they stood in the center of the road and flagged it down.

The three of them sat shivering in the back seat, Harry between the two women. The driver was a middle-aged country man with several days of stubble on a slender face that appeared neither friendly nor hostile, expressed no curiosity about how they happened to be on that remote section of a remote road, nor inquired of their destination. He simply announced: "I can get you to Twain Harte."

"That'll be fine," Harry said, feeling an urge to explain. But nothing plausible came to mind and the silence stretched past the point where unsolicited speech could be offered without self-consciousness. Once Harry thought to ask about the dozen or so rabbits occupying a narrow hutch riding on the front seat, but he was afraid to display what might be construed as phony amicability. So the three passengers sat in macabre strained silence, respecting the speechless demeanor of their host.

An hour later they stood huddled in the doorway of the village theater where a primitive lightless marquee announced: CLOS D F R EASON. Kitty fished a cigarette from her purse and struck futilely at a damp matchbook. She threw the matches down, then the cigarette, and the curbside torrents swirled them away. Harry's eyes burned. Across the street pink neon letters flickered on a dark brick façade, CAFE, evoking warmth, conversation, the homey clatter of china.

"Why can't you think what to do?" Kitty demanded.

Harry stared at the rain, beyond even his usual shrug.

"I'm starved," Alice said.

"Hey," Kitty said; her face brightened. "Hey Harry, she's still got it."

"What?" Alice said.

"The seven thousand." Kitty snatched at Alice's purse.

"No," Alice said.

"God damn it, I want that money."

Alice shook her head, smirking.

"Harry, I want that money."

"You really are sick," Alice muttered to the roar of rain.

"Harry." Kitty was shaking him now. "That's our money. We have got to have it, Harry!"

He did not want to hear. His throat ached. His lips moved, but no sound came. Kitty's face leered before him, intense, desperate. This was not her; it was all the years of frustration and defeat, crushing the bloom at her center. He put his hand gently to her face. "Don't you see?"

[ 184 ]

She brushed his hand away. Suddenly he did not know her: his compassion was gone. He wanted to withdraw into himself, to huddle on a street corner, to watch indifferently as life passed by.

"Don't you see?" he repeated.

"I see nothing but what an asshole you are!" She was close to hysteria.

"You're the asshole," Alice said.

Kitty lashed out, striking her. For a moment Alice stood, stunned by the other woman's fury. She made no sound, no defense, holding to her purse by simple instinct.

"No," Harry said, but he did not move. Headlights crept through the rain. The two women were at his feet, rolling on the sidewalk, arms thrashing. For a second that etched on his memory, he was mesmerized by the sight, both severe and comic, so bizarre as to be beyond any reaction but wonder. A gutterspout roared with collected rain. They both tugged at the purse, fists wild, sprawled in diffuse rage. He bent, and as if inserting his hands into fire, stretched his arms into their flailing. His mouth stung with sudden bruised warmth. Then he was alone, sitting, pulling his hand from his face, his fingers alive with blood.

"Harry, stop her!" He looked up to see Alice disappear under the pink neon letters into the café. "We need that money!"

He nodded.

"She's going to tell."

"No," he said.

"You're bleeding."

"It's okay."

"Harry, we'll split it. Harry—" Her voice broke. He held her. "I'm scared," she sobbed. He held her face up to the rain and brushed streaks of mud from her cheeks.

"It'll be all right," he said.

"I want to go home."

"I know."

"Tonight. Right now."

"Okay," he said.

"What will you do, Harry?"

"I'm going to get that son of a bitch."

"Oh Harry, you're such a—"

"I don't want you to leave," he said.

"I can't wait."

"Where would you go?"

A man emerged from a neighboring store, stared at them huddled there, then moved to his car. They watched his hand brush the fog from his windshield, saw him staring.

"Maybe to Lee's. I don't know."

"Who's Lee, for christ's sake?"

"A friend. Just a friend. Come on," she said. "Let's go across."

"No."

"You afraid?"

"That son of a bitch is watching."

"Let's go across. Later you can get in touch with me at Lee's. After it blows over."

He looked at her, a faint smile. "This ain't going to blow over, sweetie. Not in a long while."

"That's not what you said."

"Something didn't go right this time."

"Who are we kidding, Harry?"

"Everybody. I hope to hell it's everybody."

"Let's go," she said.

The café was brightly lit, the atmosphere thick with coffee and damp clothes, a festive hubbub of conversation. His scalp prickled when he entered, but nobody took special note of them, not even Alice sitting alone in a rear booth. They sat with her, Kitty sliding on the inside. Alice acknowledged them with a nod. The waitress dropped three menus on the table.

"Guess I'm treating," Alice said.

"Damn right," Kitty said.

"Kitty, don't," Harry said.

[ 186 ]

"I want that money, Harry." Her voice was harsh with restraint.

"It's mine," Alice said. "Harry gave it to me. We made a deal."

"I don't care what deal you made."

"Kitty—" Harry put his hand over hers. "You're not being rational. Think of what she knows."

"I don't—"

"Shh."

"Okay. Okay," she said. "I get the goddamn point."

"It's about time," Alice jeered.

As Kitty leaned across the table to spit, Harry clamped his hand over her mouth. The front door opened, bells jingling, and there was a hush, a momentary decorum: two state troopers walked in, glanced over the patrons, then sat at two spaces cleared for them at the counter. Harry's arm started to shake. Kitty's eyes rolled.

"Now cool it," he said in a harsh whisper.

The waitress stood over them, pencil poised, with a face of professional cheer. They ordered, then sat silent, their glances sparking as if in frustrated speech. Then for a time, they lost themselves in the steaming food.

The plates were cleared and Alice ordered dessert. Kitty asked the waitress for matches. The waitress pointed to the cash register.

"Honey, I'm very busy," the waitress said.

Kitty nodded. She hated that matches had become so important to her. She hated the busy waitress. She hated the police for being there.

"Harry, find out about the bus," she said softly so Alice would not hear.

"No, stay."

"I can't." Her whisper was a wail, full of a child's despair. He nodded. She turned her body and fished in her purse, frenzied. He felt her hiding something. She placed a damp packet of cigarettes on the table.

"Harry, please get me some matches, okay?"

He looked at her, the sensual mouth pursed tight, the pale blue eyes steely. Involuntarily he touched her cheek; she brushed his hand away.

"Harry, please." Her hand trembled with the cigarette.

"You really want me to walk past them?"

She nodded. He got up, hitching his shoulders, and set off with a grim rapid step, determined not to hesitate. He picked up two books of matches. One of the troopers turned and looked straight at him. Harry smiled, nodded. The trooper nodded back. Harry held up his hand displaying the matchbooks, instantly feeling the stupidity of his gesture. The trooper raised his chin and motioned. Harry picked up two extra matchbooks and placed them on the counter next to the trooper's hand.

"Do I know you?" the trooper said.

"I don't think so, sir."

"Wet enough for you?"

"Almost," Harry said.

"Thanks," the trooper said, indicating the matches.

Harry returned to the booth. Kitty was gone.

"In the bathroom," Alice said.

Harry nodded and started to shake. He hid his hands under the table.

"I gave her a thousand dollars," Alice said.

"You what?"

"Anyway, I didn't need it all. And I was worried."

"About what? What do you have to be worried about?"

Alice shrugged. "Funny, isn't it?"

"What's funny?"

"All this. It seems like a dream, but it seems it had to happen."

"I guess so," he said.

"Sugar," she said. He passed it and she poured it across her spoon. "You know, this is the biggest thing ever happened to me."

"Well, it's over," he said.

[ 188 ]

"You think so?"

When he nodded, a lighthearted laugh slipped out and Alice wagged her head in private glee.

"What's so funny?"

"All of it, I guess."

"Maybe for you."

"I'm sorry. It's just you *are* such a perfect madman."

"Thanks a lot," he said.

Kitty came from the bathroom, her hair in a scarf, her face devoid of makeup. She moved in jerky furtive motions. He had to look twice to see it was her. She did not acknowledge him, but simply walked past and out into the rain. When he reached the door, she was gone.

# 3

Alice stood in front, and with each passing car thrust her arm out. They were drenched in incessant spray torn up by passing vehicles. He could see her body shake. A familiar small blue sedan with a missing fender stopped. It was Starcrest coming back from town with groceries. Alice told the tale of Dogman's disappearance.

"No," Starcrest said. "He wouldn't do that. He wouldn't rip you off. He'll be back."

The dogs greeted them, splashing them with mud. Starcrest took them to her room through a barrage of commiserations and more assurances Dogman would soon return. They stripped off their wet clothes, shyly, their backs to one another, then climbed into ill-fitting borrowed clothing.

"You have to call your father," he said.

"Do I?"

"You have to make him believe it. They'll kill me."

"No," she said. "I won't let them."

There was a pause. "Sure. Thanks," he said.

"Grasshopper?"

"Yeah?"

"I don't think . . ."

"What?"

"I don't think you like me."

"You just don't seem to understand what a mess, what a serious mess—"

"Did you really need it that bad? I mean money isn't everything—it really isn't."

He sighed. "I don't know. I just thought if I could get out of the rut, have a chance to think who in hell I was. Shit, it sounds ridiculous . . ."

She touched his arm, shy, tentative: "Not to me."

"Ahh what d'you know? You're so young, you got everything you need."

"You think so?"

"I don't know. I'm sick of talking."

"I know where you're at, Harry. I had some shit to get away from too. So in a way you helped me. It's like you're from outer space and you don't even know it. Sometimes I feel like I'm living on two levels. I'm scared to go home. You know what they'll do? They'll fucking smother me—poor little traumatized baby. They'll love me to death. They'll make me hate them more."

He slumped onto the bed. He did not appear to have heard her: to him it had seemed like a speech, the declaration of a bored little girl too smart for her own britches. He thought: This has nothing to do with me, nothing.

She sat beside him cuddling, wanting his arm around her. "Harry," she said touching his face, and she seemed older, her face and voice transmuted. "I can't go back."

"You have to."

"I can't. I just can't." Suddenly she was a little girl; her voice crawled on his nerves.

"Stop it," he said. He reached and found the gun tucked under the mattress, exactly where he had stashed it less than twenty-four hours before. I'm living too fast. Can't take much more. Or maybe this is what happens just before you die. Like part of you knows it's over, and you're trying to get it all in.

"Harry, now's my chance. I could take off, see things. I want to go to Europe."

"Sure," he said.

"Someplace. Someplace where things are different."

"So? Your old man's got money enough."

"No, don't you see, it's not that. If I get it from them I can't do anything. This way—think of it, all those little villages. We travel cheap, just take things as they come."

He was smiling at himself: he had dreamed this dream.

"What's wrong, grasshopper?"

"Nothing."

"You don't believe it, do you?" She ran her finger across his face.

"It's not that." He examined the pistol, broke the chamber, closed it. There was a long pause.

"I guess you really don't care for me," she said.

"It's not that."

"You love her, don't you?"

He did not answer.

"Why?" she said.

"You make it all sound so simple, Alice."

"It'll blow over. I mean, if you want I'll go back and we can meet later."

He nodded. "Yeah, that's what we agreed. You go back. That way poor old Harry Keller won't get blamed." He laughed.

"You're being facetious, aren't you?"

"Facetious?"

"Yes, facetious."

"Sure, that's what I'm being."

"You make everything so difficult." She ruffled her hands through his hair.

He smiled. "Maybe I ought to just go back and turn myself in and say, gee I didn't really know what I was doing."

She thought about it, with petulant seriousness. "Maybe," she said. "You know, maybe that would be best. The old man said he'd stick up for you. I mean if he gave his word, it's good. That's one thing I'll say for him."

"You like him," he said.

[ 195 ]

"Nah. Not really. But you weren't going to keep your promise, were you? That's why the car broke down. You know that."

He shrugged. He didn't want to acknowledge anything. He wished she would go away.

"But I knew when you left me. I knew the car would break down."

"How?"

"I just did. You think it's over, don't you?"

He stood, spun the pistol on his finger; it was heavy, clumsy. I could just go crazy, he thought.

"Harry." She spoke his name softly, her hand stroking his hair. "Harry, you're going to be okay."

He snickered. "Sure."

"You can sleep with me if you want."

"How old are you anyway?"

"Seventeen."

"I mean really."

"In a week I will be. Honest."

He laughed, a quiet nervous laugh that grated his throat.

"You still think I'm trying to trick you," she said. "I never was. Even when you were driving me crazy with those handcuffs." Her face puckered, became childlike again, baffled, on the verge of tears.

"You're a strange one," he said.

She laughed, and the laughter instantly transformed into tears. He wanted to touch her, but he did not dare. Darkness moved into the room, sponging up the last light. His body began to shake, a high febrile trembling. He fell back, the pistol across his belly.

"No," he said. "It wouldn't be right."

Kitty found herself under cold neon, her nostrils burning with bus fumes. For a moment she stood blinking, clutching her purse as if tugged by some invisible assailant. She found an empty bank of telephones, but she had no change. She bought a cup of coffee in the depot confectionary and left it standing. She remembered four numbers at once, but did not know which was his. A private patrolman passed and she shuddered, hiding her face. She found Lee Sandzone's name in a tattered directory. She became frantic when a recording answered and delivered instructions in Lee's crisp slightly sardonic tones that seemed to couch certain desperate intentions; yet the very familiarity of his voice gave her something to cling to. After she started to speak, there was a click and his unrecorded voice cut in.

"Katherine?"

"Yes, Lee, I need—" Her voice quivered and broke, and the uncontrollable weeping began. He kept telling her to stay calm and asking her where she was. She laughed: laughing at his solicitude and her own inability to find her voice. She was quite startled that he seemed to care.

Finally she blubbered, half-laughing: "At the Greyhound station."

"I'll be down."

"No, please, I'll get a cab. I just wanted to know if it'd be all right?"

"Sure, sweetie. Sure."

She sneaked a hand into her purse and felt the damp, slightly greasy packets. Three thousand dollars. Better than nothing. Her eyes stung again. She was certain something was wrong with her, because never had crying been so painful: her tears were acid. Haven't eaten right, or slept. Have to take care of myself, sleep for a week.

He opened the door in his maroon velvet robe, and ushered her into the high-ceilinged foyer with its stained-glass fanlights that illumined and dimmed with the fluctuations of passing traffic.

He looked at her with devouring concern, rubbing the dark stubble on his broad face. He looks so innocent, she thought. She let him hold her, cuddling into his arms in a kind of exalted despair and terminal weariness, thinking: Daddy, Daddy, and laughing at herself before she broke into fresh tears. She could feel him flinch; he told her not to cry and offered her a drink, but she refused to let him stop holding her.

When her weeping had subsided, he took her into the living room and without asking poured her half a tumbler of whiskey. It all seemed a dream now. Even the present. Yet she had traveled from that other dream, the madder one, with another stranger she had been intimate with. So Lee did not seem so strange now. And no longer threatening. At that moment she realized she could command him, if only with a display of helplessness. Previously she had expressed her will, demanded recognition as an abused and misunderstood artist, and he had jeered at her: gently, wisecracking, but nonetheless he had jeered. And he had led her on, charmed her, pretended concern. Then he had asked her to leave. And when she returned he had sold her whatever drug she wanted, without question, at the going rate. "No discount for former concubines," he had joked, "or I'd be the most bankrupt dealer in town." She had managed to slap him then—but he

[ 198 ]

had only smirked and grabbed her, forcing her to the floor, stopping only at the last minute, his breath hammering her face. "Not even rape excites you. You're so dry I'd skin myself." She spit. He laughed and spit back. "All right, sweetie, take the goddamn dope. Just don't set foot in this house again." And that night, that very same night another dummy tries to give her a tip and gets his face busted and a week later ... She was laughing, on the edge, thinking, If I let go, if I really did, they'd send me to the nuthouse.

"You all right?" he asked.

A bit drunk, she thought. Smell it on him. Really helpless. She laughed aloud.

"What's so funny?" he asked in dead earnestness.

She played with him. "I've told you, Lee, I'm hung up. A hang-up's a hang-up, you know."

"But what's the big joke?" he insisted.

"You," she blurted.

"Me?" He seemed genuinely perplexed.

You're a softie, she thought. Under it all you're just another softie. Funny I never saw it. Fogged me over with charm. She tilted her head back and poured the drink down. She remembered the day in the sun at the lake. I'm done with sipping, she thought. Crazy ladies don't sip. Another softie. Oh god, don't feel guilty, she told herself, thinking she was going to cry. It wouldn't've worked with him.

"More," she said.

"Sure," he said. His eyes glinted. Okay, Mr. Lee Sandzone, you'll get it, but don't be too cocksure.

"You're different," he said.

She smirked. "Think so?" God, drunk already. A minute ago I wanted to sleep.

"You okay?" he said.

"Sure," she said. "I'm great. Fabulous!"

"You look better," he said. "Let's go upstairs."

"Yeah," she said, lifting her glass.

"Kathy," his voice rubbed close and intimate in her ear,

a hand on her shoulder, corralling her. What in hell, did he forget what he was going to say?

"What?"she said.

"Huh?" he said. They were near the top of the stairs. "Kathy?"

"That's me," she said with heavy irony, fighting her intoxication.

"You're something else."

She put her fingers across his mouth. Inside she was laughing. "You got no idea what I've been through," she said with no particular emphasis.

"I'd like to know."

"Maybe," she said. "But no bullshit, okay?"

He snickered. "What's that mean?"

"Okay?" she said.

"Okay," he said.

I hope I remember all this in the morning, she thought and stripped off her clothes.

When she woke, there was sun behind the heavy maroon drapes. Her head was fuzzy with residues of whiskey and dream-disturbed slumber. Her eyes darted, disoriented. Then she remembered where she was, and fell back. Have to get to a bank. But not all of it. Maybe Lee would keep some. Or put it in a deposit box. Probably think I'm a hooker. Or dealer. Call Veronica, ask her how . . .

Lee entered in the same maroon velvet robe, bearing coffee on a tray. She was surprised how glad she was to see him. He poured the coffee and lit a pipe. She shook her head. He inhaled. Then she changed her mind and took some herself. She knew then she would have to tell someone, and decided it might as well be him. After all, he was a professional: he was noted for not revealing sources. Three years back he had gone to jail rather than do it. He had made quite a name for himself.

"Lee," she said. "I've got something to tell you."

"Sure," he said, and she knew he had been waiting for her to say this.

He sat smoking, tamping the ashes and relighting the pipe, noisily sipping cup after cup of scalding coffee poured from a chrome carafe. He did not appear surprised, never questioned her veracity, only occasionally prompted her for some detail.

"Where is he?" he said.

"How should I know?"

"Back at that ranch, waiting for Dogman?"

She shrugged. He slapped his thigh and moved to the closet, letting his robe fall. He selected a body shirt and tailored trousers, then let those drop and dressed in blue denim pants and a western shirt with pearl snaps.

"What are you going to do?"

"Does he still trust you?"

"I don't know."

"I'll need a note. I'll split with you fifty-fifty, after expenses. Expenses will include what I pay him. He deserves something." Lee laughed. "Jesus, this is a goddamn goldmine."

She felt her mouth moving, felt herself shrinking into the bed. "No," she murmured.

"What?"

"No, I can't—"

"You don't like the terms? Listen, Katherine, I like you very much, but this is a big story. You realize how they've been playing this up? A goddamn abduction that maybe isn't an abduction. I mean the speculation on this is wild. They've got some old man he was friends with. And his boss. Harry left a trail a mile wide. I've loved this case from the start, and now it's blown right in. I'm on his side. Even if I hated him, I would be. The longer he lasts, the bigger the story. People are already sending money to that old stuntman, for christ's sake. He swears he did it for him and the other old folks in the building." Lee laughed riotously. "Don't you see? It's a goddamn contemporary allegory and you're in it up to your neck. You're the crowning jewel, Katherine. But they can't touch you."

She was shaking her head. He sat beside her. "Hey," he said caressing her. "Hey, take it easy—"

"Oh Lee," she said and began to cry. He held her. Oh you motherfucker. Don't let me go.

When she had stopped crying, she wrote a note of introduction. It was tear-stained. It would be the only note Harold Keller would ever receive from Katherine Ann Kruse. When she wrote it, she did not think it was a lie. In it, she declared, quite simply, her love for him. She said Lee Sandzone would help him. She believed it.

Three hours after she wrote it, Lee Sandzone opened it in a hired two-engine plane about to touch down at the Stockton airstrip. He read it, then resealed it in another envelope. He was smiling.

Harry saw the unfamiliar car, then the unfamiliar figure emerge from it. He climbed down from the platform in the oak where he kept his grim vigil for the rusty gray sedan; he had been there for hours, the pistol laid across his lap, sometimes blowing riffs on his harmonica.

Half a dozen people greeted the stranger; he was dressed in blue jeans, a neatly tailored shirt with black piping and pearl snaps. He greeted them warmly in return, patting the dogs with ostentatious familiarity. They noticed Harry circling toward the barn, his nonchalant gait betraying a certain haste. When he climbed into the barn, chickens fluttered away in wild disruption. The interior suddenly brightened with dusty spires of light as a cloud moved from the sun. A roan mare, known as Rusty, snorted in her stall and nosed his shoulder as he passed. He climbed a narrow ladder into the loft redolent with hay that had sat too long. Light leaked through the roof like stars punched in a firmament. Is this me? he said, unsure whether he had spoken aloud. He looked at the gun. He pressed its muzzle to his forehead.

The barn seemed to make a noise, a pleasant music. He pulled the gun away and took the harmonica from his pocket, and put it to his mouth: the faint brassy taste was comforting. He started, hearing someone on the ladder. He dug into the hay, insects springing out in clouds, then turned and peered out at the open trapdoor. A hand emerged, bearing an envelope. A child's hand. He let the pistol drop. The child smiled. He had forgotten her name.

"From the man," she said. "He's a friend of the lady that was here. He wants to talk to you." The girl gave a little shrug, smiling, having completed her mission.

Harry nodded. "Okay," he said. "You better go."

She curtsied and giggled, then disappeared down the ladder.

He sat in the half-rotten hay and read the note three times. His shoulders began to shake.

> *Trust him. I told him everything. He wants to help you. And it will help me too. I really do love you. Sorry it couldn't work out.*

Bullshit. He cursed softly through his tears.

The man was waiting outside, perched on a stump that had rolled off a mound of unsplit firewood. His head was leaned back, his face bronze in the setting sun, looking cocksure and self-possessed, an expression Harry had often tried to assume. The man was Harry's age, or a few years older. He did not deign to give his attention until Harry was standing over him.

"Lee Sandzone," the man said. "Maybe you've heard of me?" He extended his hand; the grip was warm, even respectful.

"I haven't," Harry said.

"That's all right. If you had you'd know you're not talking to a slouch. I'm behind you. A hundred percent. I've always been for the underdog. I've been one myself."

"I don't know what you want," Harry said.

Sandzone placed a hand on Harry's shoulder. Harry wanted to shrug away, but he let the hand stay.

"Let's walk," Lee said.

They turned down the pair of ruts that crossed the field heading toward the pond. On the way Sandzone told Harry what he wanted: in short, it was exclusive rights to Harry's story. He offered two thousand in cash as a good-faith gesture; it happened to be cash Lee Sandzone had given Kitty a check for.

Harry felt a hot surge rise in his chest; his feet were light against the damp earth, and an unspecified forlornness moved in his blood, the same feeling blues music sometimes gave him. He knows they're going to get me, he thought. He's cashing in. Kitty too.

Sandzone stopped walking and looked at Harry's face as if he divined something. He shook his head with theatrical sympathy.

"Harry, no matter what happens, you're going to need money, and Katherine is going to need money. I tell you the time is ripe for someone like you. A lot of people out there are hurting. They're going to identify, man. Believe me."

"It's all over," Harry said sullenly.

"Ahh hell, pal, I know you're in a fix. I know the pressure is on. But you got to tell your side. They're already sending money to the old man."

"What?"

"Potter—he defended you, Harry. Said you did it for him. And all the old folks in the building. Said you did it to get the down payment so the damned rents wouldn't drive them to their graves. They got the interview with him sitting on that ratty old sofa all decked out in his western getup. I think he was hamming it up a bit, if you want my opinion."

The man's words washed over him, stirring up fresh absurdities. Finally Harry began to smile. The man stopped talking. "What is it?"

"He really thinks I did it for him?"

"I honestly think he does."

"I did mention it once," he said. "That we should get together and buy the building and fix it up the way we wanted."

"You know how the news ratings are going to go up. I

mean you can feel the heartthrob—because it's genuine. Oh there'll be the intellectual pisspots who'll decry this as exploitation, but it's life, man—it's to America what the tragedies were to the Greeks. Let's not kid ourselves. You're an intelligent man, Harry. That's what makes this interesting. You aren't just some freaked-out crackpot. You made a conscious decision. It has class."

"Thanks," Harry murmured.

"Yes pal, it does. That's why I want you to give this interview. Not just for you and Katherine and the old man, but for all the millions of others out there. Christ, Harry, you could start a revolution. Did you ever think of that?"

Despite himself he was caught in the man's enthusiasm, even while he distrusted it, sensed something distasteful in it; like someone suddenly caught in a circus who does a simple somersault and the crowd goes wild.

"Harry, I got a camera crew on the way up. Just two guys, very trustworthy."

"No," Harry said.

"Listen, Harry," Sandzone said softly with a direct stare, "this is too big for me to pass up, you understand?"

Harry's stomach began to vibrate in acute little quivers.

"Harry, the longer you stay loose, the better. In fact if you get away and disappear altogether, that's what's best. That's the stuff myths are made of. Besides, if they nab you, they'll never make it stick. Even Fisk wants to cool it. And the girl—what's her name?"

"Alice."

"Alice went along with it. Don't you see?"

"I guess so," Harry said.

"Put it here," Sandzone said and took Harry's hand. They shook. At that moment a flock of goats broke around them, chased by a band of boys carrying primitive bows and spears.

At shortly after seven o'clock that evening, Lee Sandzone entered the pre-twilight gloom of the barn on the old Tomlin place, that farmhouse and its various outbuildings on forty acres of western Sierra foothills now known by its inhabitants as the Rainbow Ranch. Harry watched him through a hole in the loft floor. Behind him came two men bearing aluminum cases, and behind them several citizens of the ranch carrying lighting stands and rolls of cable.

It was Harry who had suggested the interview be done in the barn, and Lee Sandzone had readily agreed, admiring Harry's theatrical intuition: what more melodramatic spot for a fugitive to be questioned.

Harry watched them setting up the equipment. Alice hung over his shoulder, her breath nervous with anticipation. He had got used to her now, had even come to take comfort in her company; at times his aloneness became exalted, but the feeling would not sustain itself, and Alice was always there with her precocious understanding for him to wallow in.

"Are you nervous?" she whispered.

"What d'you think?"

"You don't seem it," she said.

Below them the lights popped on, flooding a circular area with magisterial intensity. Lee Sandzone came up the ladder into the loft. "It's set," he said.

Harry stared at him without speaking.

"Hey, my friend, we're waiting."

Harry shook his head.

"What's that mean?"

"I don't want to," Harry said.

"What do you mean you don't want to?" Lee put a reassuring arm over Harry's shoulder. "They'll be crying for you, Harry. You got to. This story is bigger than both of us, don't you see?"

"Leave him alone," Alice said quietly.

"Harry," Lee said. "Now's your chance to tell your side, just like you wanted."

"Ahh, what's the difference," he said, and pulled a knitted ski mask over his face in a gesture even he recognized as futile in its attempt to preserve the shreds of his anonymity. But despite its absurdity it seemed proper, expected. And it would hide his fear, not only from the anonymous viewers but from the woman who had sent this man to question him.

He descended the ladder and stood blinded by the hot lights, a surreal apparition, his hands crossed in front of him, chickens meandering between his legs. There was a smell of hot metal and a rich resonance of animal and hay. Dust motes drifted in the light beams. The bemused faces of goats peered forth from their stalls. A bearded man came forward and clipped a microphone to his shirt. Then Lee Sandzone was standing beside him, speaking toward the camera in solid tones, as if slightly awed by his own voice:

"Behind the simplified headlines and superficial media reports are real human beings. Very rarely are those accused of a crime given a chance to tell their own story, and even those given the opportunity rarely are able or willing to. A criminal by his nature is secretive, paranoid, often inarticulate. In Doctor Cloud we have an exception: an intelligent, self-educated man, he could hardly be called the criminal type. Yet he was driven to take from those he felt had too much. This was not an organized revolutionary or terrorist act as has been reported, but simply the existential rebellion of one man against his intolerable position in a system that creates expectations it does not always deliver. Hank Cloud is a man who had the courage, not only to act, but the greater courage to come forth and clarify the meaning of those acts. This reporter does not condone criminal or violent behavior, no matter what the circumstances, but he does encourage those in any walk of life who have the courage to speak the truth."

Sandzone stepped aside to a slight shuffling of feet and furry noises from throats, a cough or two, a snort from the mare. Harry listened to these noises, sweating under the mask.

"Go ahead, Harry," Sandzone said. "Just tell it from the beginning."

He was shaking his head, and it seemed to him he had been shaking his head, mouth frozen, jaws clenched, for years: this was the primeval intractable gesture given from birth.

"It's okay, Harry."

"Do they have to be here?"

"Who?"

"Behind the lights."

"Harry, there's nobody."

"I feel them," he said.

Alice's whisper came from outside the pool of light that seemed to have caught him like a moth. "Harry, he's right. There's nobody but us."

Lee entered the light and took Harry aside. "Listen, Harry, as soon as it's done we're getting you out of here. Straight to Mexico. Your own private air service. All part of the deal. I got friends down there will put you up. This interview is your ticket out. Remember that. Your ticket out."

Harry nodded, and fluttered back into the light. He paced the perimeter, then he stopped, faced the camera, and began to speak; his voice was somber but strong.

At seven o'clock Dan Pritchard, duly elected sheriff of Sonoma County, oversaw the towing of an abandoned convertible with half a dozen holes in its hood, which he swore were caused by a firearm. Why one would want to shoot up an automobile like that puzzled him. If the holes had been in the trunk, it would have been plausible, especially with the discovery of a body.

At 7:30 he stopped by Hoosicks's tavern; it was a good place to eat and catch up on local gossip. The only customer was Mildred, though it was early even for her. She sat sullenly over her beer watching the television set above the bar. Pritchard exchanged civilities with Hoosicks, who went in back to prepare the sheriff's supper himself. When Pritchard looked down the long mahogany bar, Mildred waved at him as if to say: don't bother me. He smiled and sipped at a watery cola.

He was halfway through his meal, still musing on the bullet-ridden convertible, when Mildred perked up; her mouth opened and she pointed at the television screen.

"The sound," she stammered. "Turn it up."

Hoosicks ignored her. Pritchard glanced up at the screen. A man, vaguely familiar to him, came onto the front steps of a columned residence, spoke a few words to a clamor of people that looked like press, then quickly returned into the house. The scene changed to an old man in a stained

Stetson who spoke directly at the lens, nodding gravely, his eyes rolling. Pritchard remembered this man as the father of the man who had abducted the Fisk girl. He ruminated on what it must be like to crack a big case like that. He motioned to Hoosicks to turn the sound up.

"That's her," Mildred shrieked.

Pritchard smiled.

"That's her, I tell ya!" She slipped off her stool and stumbled forward several steps. "Don'tcha remember that little gal with that hippie fella with the dogs?"

"Paul?"

"Yeah, Paul and that girl. I knew I'd seen her somewheres."

"Sure, Mildred," Hoosicks said. "Have another beer, kid."

"Sheriff," Mildred said.

"Now calm down."

"And that fella. Look!" She gestured toward the screen. "Don't he look a bit like?"

"Calm down," the barman said.

Pritchard got the story from Hoosicks while Mildred drunkenly harangued her certainty that the Fisk kidnapper had been there just two or three nights before. He finished his supper quickly and set off for the old Tomlin place, which he himself remembered visiting as a boy. Not that he was sure there was anything in this drunken talk, but it was an excuse to go see what that bunch of weirdos was up to. Damn, it'd be fine, he thought. I hope the hell he is there. Then something clicked in his mind. He called on the radio and twenty minutes later received a report confirming his hunch: the car with the bullet holes answered the description of the car driven by the kidnapper. He decided to round up a couple of deputies and rendezvous in Twain Harte. His pulse lifted. All the way to the village he pondered on why the man had found it necessary to shoot up a perfectly good automobile.

A wind had risen and cool drafts wafted through the loose planking, so the barn itself seemed to rustle. Occasionally a gust would tear loose a shingle. There was a distant rumble of thunder. The goats began a bleating chorus to Harry's narrative. He went blindly on. They're going to get me, he thought. They're going to shoot me down like a dog. But it only made him want to howl harder, to force his feelings into words that would somehow be understood.

"I wanted to do something, to make something, but all there was, was this fixing things to have enough money to go on fixing things, and even what I was fixing I hated, all those TVs babbling things that didn't make sense. I didn't want to end up being one of them. I saw them every day, sitting in front of their TVs like mummies."

A throttled sob lurched from him, and he momentarily turned his head from the camera.

"Weren't you taking this all rather personally?" Lee Sandzone asked from outside the circle of light.

Harry whirled in sudden rage. "Sure. Sure I was!"

"Why didn't you do something different?"

"Sure, why not? Ahh hell, if you don't know, you don't know. All they ever want to see is some paper saying who you are and what you're worth. I never had any paper."

The barn shook with a long crackling roll of thunder. Rain came through the roof, pocking little craters on the dusty floor.

"What exactly did you want the money for?"

"I don't know. Maybe it was just for time enough to get my breath. Everything was such a rush I couldn't think straight."

"Wouldn't some call that rather selfish?"

"How in hell can I answer that?" Harry said.

"In your own words," Lee Sandzone said.

Harry laughed. "No matter what I say I look bad. Hell, if you don't grab and you don't have money, nobody even looks at you except to see what they can use you for. 'Course if you're big enough, you don't need to justify anything. You can rip everybody off and nobody touches you. But if somebody like me gets uppity—but see, you got me already. You're going to say it's sour grapes."

"Nobody's passing judgment."

"Why should you? You're cashing in. I don't blame you. I don't blame them. I don't blame anybody. I was just trying to get a little too. Only I wasn't good enough. The moral is, whatever you do, be a professional. Shit, this sounds like a goddamn speech. I hate it. It's not what I mean."

"Harry, I want to get back to why you needed the money."

"I told you I wasn't any good at this."

Sandzone smiled, cleared his throat. "You *did* need the money, didn't you? It wasn't simply a lark."

Harry stopped pacing. "You trying to make a fool of me?"

"Of course not. Please, tell us why you needed the money."

His voice was obliterated by another roll of thunder; when it had trailed off, Sandzone asked him to begin again.

"Where was I?"

"You said you didn't want the money for its own sake."

"Yes," Harry said. "It wasn't the money. It was the treadmill. See, there was something in me that couldn't take it. A born weakness, I guess. I was a worker, all right. Like they say, worked my butt off to stay poor. Now why in hell did it have to be so pointless to me? Answer me that."

"I'd rather hear your explanation."

"I haven't got any. All I know is it drove me nuts. TV sets day after day. Just the smell of them used to make me sick. And half the time I did feel like a criminal, I mean those daily little rip-offs replacing parts that didn't need it to make the quotas, or telling some poor old lady it was going to cost her a fortune to fix her set so she'd be better off getting a reconditioned one—and we'd fix up the old one and sell it to the next old lady for a nice fat profit. And even when we did it straight, we'd charge them twenty bucks an hour to fix a damn machine that was going to spend ninety percent of the time feeding them a bunch of crap anyway. . . . Shit, it's just words. It's dead because I don't know the right words—you see, with no money, when you're always scrounging, ninety-nine percent look at you like you're a loser. Not outward, but inside they secretly feel you're exactly where you deserve to be. Funny thing, the other losers can't afford to care about you either. They're scared to care, because if it means getting ahead, most of them'll cut your throat. And underneath they think you'd do the same, and be a fool not to, not just a fool, but a loser. It's a vicious circle. I wanted out of that. Don't you see?"

"Maybe you could elaborate—"

"You got to see! You got to!"

"Just calm down," Lee Sandzone said. "We'll edit this out."

"No," he said. "I don't want this out."

"You'll look like a fool."

"I don't give a damn," Harry said. "Let me. Let me look like a fool."

Sandzone exchanged glances with the cameraman, who gestured back indicating there was five minutes of film left in the magazine.

"You seriously don't think what you did was wrong?" Sandzone asked.

Harry let forth a breathless desperate laugh and tore the

mask off. His face was flushed, manic, almost comedic with anger. "The only thing I did wrong was I blew it. I was a chump!"

"How do you feel about it now?" Sandzone said. "Do you regret what you've done?"

At first he did not appear to hear. There was another roll of thunder. He paced the circle of light.

"Harry, I wondered if you regretted what you had done?"

Rain dripped steadily through the roof into muddy pools. Harry spoke quietly. "You see, if I could have just closed my eyes and gone on day after day getting the paycheck, getting drunk on weekends, paying the rent, paying off the boss, overlooking the poor scared old ladies and fixing the goddamn TVs and keeping my mouth shut, everything shut, but I was eating myself alive, I was dying, I tell you!"

"But Harry, there are millions—"

"But I'm me! You get that? I'm me!" He stopped and all sound, all movement, seemed momentarily suspended. Inside he struggled for what he wanted to say, but knew it was too complex, variegated, and confused ever to be articulated. Even if he had had the words, he could not have made known what it was he wanted to say, because in part it was not solely a series of events he had witnessed and experienced and could narrate in words, but a condition that had become evident in his slouch, his wrinkles, in the anxiety that periodically flared. He knew, but did not know how to say, that the ultimate source of his anger was something beyond the petty injustices he named. It was a deeper betrayal: the theft of hope, and with it the dignity he had come to see and had tried to acknowledge in others as a right of birth. Had he been able, he would even have acknowledged that this sense of essential dignity was perhaps a romance, perhaps grandiose, and he would have admitted it counted for little in the scheme of things. For it was power that won out. Of this he was sure.

Lee Sandzone stepped into the light: "Harry, I'm not sure our audience will—"

"Give it back," Harry said. "This isn't right."

"Take it easy now, Harry." Lee Sandzone held up his hand as if to ward him off.

"It's wrong, it's a lie, all a goddamn lie! Nobody'll understand!"

"Harry, it's your ticket out."

Harry shook his head and lunged for the camera. The newsman deftly tripped him, sending him sprawling, rolling through the muddy puddles. The next instant something inside the barn changed: dust and straw swirled. A voice called out: "The cops!"

"Kill the lights," Sandzone said and turned to address Harry, but he was gone.

He tore at the loose hay, making a burrow into the mow. Alice worked beside him. He pushed her in and crawled after. He pulled hay back into the opening. Then they waited, feeling the change in pressure as the barn doors again opened and closed. There were voices under the furious tattoo on the roof. He began to scratch at the vermin invading his clothes. A profound panic welled up in him. Then her breath, small and hot against his shoulder, like a lamp. Her fingers moved in his hair. He was about to cry. Her mouth pushed hotly against his. He held her.

The dogs started to bark, and straining he could make out curses followed by laughter. There was another change in pressure. He scooted deeper into the hay. Through the steady drumming he heard voices come nearer, up the ladder. He felt them looking. Now he actually welcomed the distraction of the vermin. The floorboards creaked. His breath stopped. There were two of them. One of them kicked at the hay: "Somebody's been up here."

"Yeah, I can imagine what they was up to."

There was a rough virile guffawing.

"Does Pritchard really think he's here, or has he just got ants in his pants?"

[ 217 ]

"I believe he does." There was another kick at the hay. "Jesus, look at them bugs, Jake. I wouldn't want my ass in that mess, no matter what was in there with me."

"Pritchard wants a look-around in daylight. Keep someone here all night."

"Shit, let the old man stay."

The voices moved away. Then there was only the rain and their lungs gulping air in the close scurrying darkness.

Rain. Darkness. Mud. The violent whipping of trees illumined by stark flashes; her face, pale, narrow, her hair dripping. Why was she following him? Perhaps it was what used to be called destiny? He had never believed it, but now he felt it. He was glad she was there, yet it was wrong she should be tramping through the stormy night woods, soaked to the skin, with a fugitive who would soon die. She had no reason to. It made no sense. But he was too tired to fight her off.

It was the woman Starcrest who led them. They clung to each other, three humans frail in the tumult. She led them on a path to the asphalt road below the ranch. She had offered this guidance for no reason he could fathom, as if she too had been caught by some subsidiary thread of his destiny. Yet it was these two women, strangers to one another, who seemed to sense a direction in this mad unfurling. And the reasons, the superficial reasons he had tried to formulate that had led to his standing at the threshold of a pool of light in the storm-racked barn telling his story, were infinitely deeper and more complex than he could guess. Yet most of life seemed to be carried out on the surface. I want to understand, I want to know where I belong.

For a fraction of a second lightning burned the image of the rainy path onto his eyes. This moment of illumination was perhaps all one could expect. The moment of seeing that dissolved into half-sight, a faded photograph of insight. It was a shock, this illumination. He almost didn't want it to come; yet he yearned for each flash and the subsequent thunderous aftermath that ran through him, made him part of this storm. He remembered the night—it seemed eons ago, from a previous lifetime—when she had slipped under him in the loft of the cabin and released herself to him: one brief moment: a mere lightning flash.

They slid down a steep embankment, and careered out onto the road. A few yards to the north he saw the ruby lights, made out the hump of the little sedan that belonged to Starcrest. His head was choked with gratitude; but words were not enough and made him ashamed.

"Take this," he said and thrust a wad of bills amounting to over five hundred dollars into her hand. "I'll need the car awhile. Give me a week. I'll let you know where I leave it."

There was a frantic series of embracings, then he was behind the wheel, his hands on the unfamiliar controls; he moved them, testing, then the sedan lurched away leaving Starcrest standing in the downpour.

He wiped the windshield with his palm and hunched forward to see through the opaque relentless rain that bounded off the asphalt and hammered the roof, leaking around the windows; he could feel the storm permeating everything, sinking into the soil, to the roots, the little fingers of plants drinking, and he felt an urge to a gay madness.

"Get something good on the radio," he said.

"It doesn't work," she said.

He fumbled the harmonica out of his pocket, picked out pieces of straw. They passed through a town. Only the bars were open, neon beckoning. He stopped and purchased beer, feeling that reckless calm that lies at the heart of danger too intense to be acknowledged.

"The way you play, it's like you're talking," she said. "It'll be beautiful in Mexico, grasshopper. Nobody'll bother us there."

"Sure," he said. "It'll be fine." And for the moment, he meant it. He tipped his beer, then blew a tune, slow and long in his blood, the brass reeds pulsing with the storm.

Early Wednesday morning, Nathaniel Fisk left his cottage at the Halcyon Days Retreat and returned to his residence on June Street where his car was mobbed by microphones and lenses. The senator refused to answer any questions, and in deference to his haggard face, most of the press respected his silence. He spoke briefly with his wife, then retired to his rarely used private study, where he tried to occupy himself with paperwork. At seven o'clock that evening, he picked up the telephone and accepted charges on a collect call.

"Thank god," he said.

"We got hung up."

"We? Where are you, Alice?"

"At a phone booth."

"For god's sake where?"

"I'm all right. I'm coming home on my own, so please just let me for once do it my way. I'm absolutely fine."

"Alice, you've got to tell me what's going on!"

"The money got stolen. Our car broke down. All kinds of problems. I'll tell you about it later. Just don't panic. Really, it was worth it. Sorry about the money."

"My god, Alice, you sound so—"

"Tell Mother I'm fine."

"Alice, wherever you are I want you to go straight to the police—"

"I've got to go now, Daddy. Of course you know I love

you and I'm sorry you've had to go through all this, but really, can't you write it off your taxes or something."

"Please Allie, you're being ridiculous. I just wish you'd tell me where—"

"You'll see me tomorrow sometime. I just don't want anybody to make a big deal. I'm A-okay. Now just one more thing, Daddy, you got to keep your promise about not pressing charges. Otherwise I'm going to say it was all my idea. That'll be very embarrassing, Daddy. I got to know him pretty well and—"

"My god, daughter, if you've been having relations—"

"Don't be ridiculous. It's just I know you gave your word and it's because of that he's let me go. I just need a little time to kind of think things out, before the cops and all that. You got to promise."

"All right, Alice, all right."

"Oh Daddy, I could hug you."

"But the law is the law. They might not dismiss everything, just on my say-so."

"Don't cross me, Daddy."

"Now Alice, I want you to go directly to the local police, wherever you are."

"I'll see you late tomorrow, Daddy."

"Alice. Alice answer me!" There was no response. The line hummed empty in his ear.

When his wife woke and he gave her the news she immediately broke into uncontrollable weeping that continued in fits and starts throughout the evening. At ten o'clock he left her under heavy sedation and returned to his study where once again he tried to bury himself in the abstract details of a piece of legislation. His eyes moved over words that left no impression. A thought erupted, formed not from the intellect and composed not so much of words as raw feeling: for a moment, the senator was certain the confused television repairman had accomplished as much with his life as the senator had with his own. For years Fisk had attempted to wield the hard-won tools of power and control with a belief, carefully hidden from his colleagues, in the possibility of righting the very wrongs Cloud had so clumsily invoked as the motives for his crime. Now the senator felt wasted, betrayed.

He got up and without conscious intent found himself walking past the master bedroom to the eastern wing of the house where Alice had lived in monklike isolation ever since she had turned thirteen. Even when the authorities had combed the place, he had not entered her room. When he did so now, he realized it was for the first time in years. He did not turn on the light. For a moment he thought he could feel her presence, and his eyes burned. Suddenly he felt like crying. Of late he had felt on the verge so many times, had even allowed a few stingy tears.

The thought that he might start to cry so disturbed him, he left the room in the futile belief that this departure in itself would eliminate all urge to emotion. He returned to his study and felt momentarily bolstered by his own rather idealized portrait dominating one wall. He turned to his father's portrait, painted years earlier by the same artist, and was again swept by a yearning he scorned as grotesquely sentimental. He quickly poured a drink and switched on the television set, aware that the man who had fixed it had become Alice's abductor. As if in answer to this awareness, the screen illumined with an image of Harry Keller's face; a washed-out and detailless photograph from a driver's license or employee's identification card, it could have been almost any reasonable-looking young male. The photograph dissolved to picture someone in a ski mask pacing a circle of light. There was a noise of thunder and strange bleating sounds. The person spoke in low earnest tones, the voice jumping out at the senator with startling familiarity.

"... the treadmill ... I wanted more. I took my chances ... nothing to blame ... it just kind of happened ... the world makes its own measure, and if you don't fit ..."

"A circus," the senator said aloud.

*"The worst moment? I don't know. I was scared the whole time. Really scared. But one of the worst things was selling my bird. . ."*

"Pitiful," the senator whispered.

On the screen the man tore his mask off. *"I blew it. I was a chump!"*

"You sure as hell did, didn't you," the senator muttered.

*"You see, if I could have just closed my eyes and gone on day after day . . ."*

The senator felt contempt quicken in his belly, and he all but turned away from the screen as the man catalogued his petty personal ills which he intimated drove him to crime. The interviewer, a man Fisk remembered having had a run-in with a few years earlier, intoned Keller's personal history, exploiting, and possibly outright fabricating, anecdotes about Keller's upbringing in orphanages and foster homes, and mentioning in a self-serving way the man's military service including duty during the height of the war.

By this time the senator had achieved what was for him a rare state of mawkish intoxication. Several times he pushed himself up to turn off the set but each time found himself caught in the man's monologue. His original contempt, he realized, was not so much for the man himself as for what he perceived to be the media's glorification of the entire mundane event. On several occasions, the senator found himself on the verge of a dizzying compassion evoked not by the man's position but by some quality in the man himself. He actually entertained the thought that had Cloud kept to the straight and narrow he might have had that charisma that makes a man successful in politics. But before he allowed this drunken empathy to overwhelm him, he reinstated the contempt of the man-of-position for the petty extortionist and buttressed it with the anger of the outraged father.

The program was finally brought to a close with a montage of photographs and freeze-frames of Keller's face in various demeanors from military deadpan to wrath to outright

[ 224 ]

laughter, his voice stammering: *"If I could have just closed my eyes . . ."* The senator raised his glass and in a tone not entirely purged of tenderness, spoke to the man on the screen. "Christ man, why'd you have to be such a damn fool?" The senator laughed in repudiation of his own gesture, and rose to pour himself another drink.

The road had become his breath. The night they fled the ranch, it rained without stopping, and all night he drove across the great central valley, then onto an obscure ill-kept highway that wound across the coastal range toward the sea. Halfway down the western slope, fog obliterated the road. An hour, then two, passed without them sighting any human landmark or encountering another vehicle. This sightless traveling lent an eerie isolation and a sense of arrested time that mirrored his mental landscape. Although he in no sense felt out of danger, he felt immune to it; he had passed beyond paranoia into a kind of fatalistic peace, so now his mind lay softly at rest. It was as if all his uncontrollable desperation had been annealed by the recording of his clumsy articulations in the barn. He thought of the anonymous mass of viewers, a few of whom might recognize him as the man who had come to repair the machine they now watched, might even recall the few moments he may have spent trying to amuse them. His awkward speech might evoke a ripple of sympathy, even understanding, but it would be offset by an even greater wave of contempt. He could not say he valued one above the other, or that either would be right. And while some would glorify and others condemn, the majority he saw as being indifferent—and perhaps this was the proper response. For what had he to do with them, or they him? Yet he knew this was a lie, or felt it so. For one of his curses had been the sense—whether illusory or not—of a terrible in-terconnectedness.

There were no markings on the road, and at times the potholed asphalt was peppered with loose rock. Though he felt the need to vent his thoughts, he and Alice had hardly spoken, and he had done nothing to encourage conversation. It wasn't that he distrusted her confidence, he simply sensed it would be unkind to share any more of himself with her. But when she outlined her grand plan of escape in tones of awesome seriousness, he listened with bemused patience that was not entirely without belief. It was all wonderfully simple, in Alice's view. They would commandeer her father's yacht and sail to Mexico. This could be done without force, for she was on intimate terms with the young man who captained the boat, and her father would not miss it for weeks, if at all, since he rarely went aboard. She would first return home, pick up her passport and placate her parents, then return to their rendezvous spot and pick him up. They would drive to San Pedro and tell Sal her father had ordered the Mexican cruise to give her time to recuperate from her ordeal and avoid the press.

"Sounds good," he said.

"Why don't you believe me?" she said.

"Part of me does," he said, and when he searched him-self, he was convinced it was true.

"Go with the part that does."

"Let's not talk," he said.

"Sometimes I think you want to be caught," she said. "Maybe she was right. Maybe you are a loser."

"I don't see what that has to do with it."

"You wouldn't."

"No," he said. "I don't want to get caught."

"They'd put you away."

"But I'd live through it," he said.

"Shit, why do I even care about you," she said.

"I didn't ask you to," he replied.

It was close to dawn when he found a pullout and stopped. When he killed the engine, they could hear the surf working the rocks far below, its violence remote, almost serene.

"What are you thinking?" she said.

"Nothing."

"You can't think nothing."

"Maybe I was wondering how it will end," he said.

"You'll be happy. With me. In Mexico."

"You know what I wanted?" he said.

"What?"

"No, it's too—"

"Too what? Corny?"

"Yes."

"I want to know."

"Go to sleep," he said and crawled into the back seat, taking the keys.

"I want to know," she demanded.

"I need to think about it," he said and she sensed in his tone a stubbornness equal to her own, and at the same time a tacit promise to tell her, so she made no further protest. After several minutes his voice nudged her from the edge of sleep. He spoke quickly and quietly, as if to himself. "I want to leave something beautiful behind."

"You already have," she said easily. He started to speak, then stopped. He thought for some reason that to thank her would be an insult. He lay awake a time watching the fog press the windows, listening to the lengthening of her breath.

It was already late afternoon when they woke to a slow steady rain and continued south on the narrow tortuous coast road that clung to palisades hundreds of feet above the Pacific. They negotiated slides and occasionally stopped to eat at a deserted vista point, solemnly chewing the cold food provided by the Rainbow Ranch. When at last they found a public telephone, she called home, briefly explained her delay in returning but refused to give her whereabouts, and demanded her father use all his influence to call off the hunt. She winked at Harry, affirming their conspiracy. Harry turned away.

As they drove on, he could feel Los Angeles pulling him. There was no reason for him to return, other than his flimsy promise to Alice to follow through with her plan. But there was a need beyond reason, a need he had as yet not recognized, and perhaps did not dare to.

An hour after the call, the first speed-limit sign flared out of the darkness. He slowed, cringing under the mercury vapor lamps of a seaside town that littered the shore of a broad bay. On the far side of the bay, a carnival had been erected, its transient glitter splashing reflections over the water. She whispered in his ear: "Oh let's go." When he protested, she assaulted him with an intense tantrum of pouting that took him by surprise, for he had forgot the part of her that remained a willful child. So partly out of guilt, and partly because he saw no reason not to, and in some small part because he shared her sense of fun despite the absurd danger it posed, he acquiesced.

They entered the gaudy whirl arm in arm. After an hour it exhausted him. He wanted quiet. He wanted to get on to whatever was waiting for him, the force that urged him southward. Then sleep. A long sleep in a place peaceful and green, without people, without billboards, where nothing would beckon but wind, water, trees.

The merry-go-round lost momentum, the rise and fall slowing. She was laughing. He wanted to laugh with her. He stepped off, weaving, dizzy.

"I can't take any more," he said.

"Oh look," she said, and pointed to a booth where glass plates rested on the heads of mammoth stuffed dogs. "I want one."

"It's a cheat," he said.

"Ahh grasshopper, please. I want to have fun."

He handed her a bill. She threw handful after handful of dimes that bounded off the glass plates while the barker wheedled. Mesmerized, he watched the coins fall, to be swept up and thrown again. She urged him to throw. He shook his head. She pushed the coins into his hand.

"You've got luck, I can tell."

In the background a din of screams and moving machinery, accelerating engines, rising and falling. All over the dying carnival money being tossed. Tears came to his eyes. Still he threw. In a corner of the booth an old woman, perhaps the barker's mother, sat in a wheelchair staring across the field of moving lights. Beside her a transistor radio bleated out the news. He listened to the report without changing the rhythm of his tosses, receiving the information almost without feeling, as though it had nothing to do with him.

*El Dorado County, California. Late this afternoon, the badly burned body of an unidentified man thought to be the Fisk kidnapper was found in an automobile by sheriff's deputies. Apparently the man failed to negotiate a turn and crashed into a ravine. The charred remains of an estimated sixty thousand dollars was recovered from the trunk. Unconfirmed reports indicate Alice Fisk had been released by her abductor prior to the accident. . . .*

Alice gave no indication of having heard. He continued to toss coins without aim, the stack of sweaty silver melting out of his cupped palm. He heard her squeal, then she was embracing him. The barker announced with cheerless enthusiasm: "Yes folks, we got ourselves a winner. Right here, the pretty little lady with the platinum hair."

"I knew you'd do it, grasshopper. I knew you would!"

She insisted they make a photograph, a talisman of their

change in luck. They entered the booth, closed the curtains. She sat in his lap, the oversized dog between her legs. They faced the dark glass. The strobe flashed. Startled . . . smirk . . . kiss . . . good-bye . . . The machine whirred. The pictures dropped.

The stuffed dog sat on the back seat. Harry drove with a half-smile on his face, thinking, So this is resignation.

"Grasshopper, it's funny, this has been so much fun," she said, examining the string of four photographs.

"Yeah," he said.

"I know what you mean now," she went on, babbling with boisterous certainty. "Nobody would understand. You could tell them till the day you die."

"Yeah, the mistake is expecting anyone to."

"But sometimes it just happens," she said. "You don't even try, and someone understands."

Traffic thickened. The road swelled to four lanes, and though he was still a hundred miles from the city he could sense the impetus of movement toward it. To keep himself awake he rolled down the window, drinking in night ocean air. Beside him the girl slept wrapped in a blanket, her mouth slightly open, her face bronzed, her pale hair moving in the wind. Such a beautiful creature, he thought.

He passed through another coastal town and fear flared in him, the old fear he thought he had almost dismissed: that he would be caught, or worse, shot down, his only legacy a headline and blood on the cold asphalt.

The night wind could no longer keep him alert. He realized how little he had slept since the night they had left Los Angeles, and with the realization nervous fatigue seemed to overpower him; so when he saw the roadside area, despite its overpopulation of bulky recreational vehicles, he pulled off. He found a place to park and they hung odd bits of clothing over the windows to obscure the glare of headlights from the adjacent highway, then curled under a blanket in a chaste seeking of warmth.

It was almost noon when Harry woke from his exhausted slumber and blinked at the sunlight penetrating their den. Before they got under way, he urged her to call home again, and Alice pretended to comply while he visited the restroom.

It was an intense summer day, the sea air blowing in its hints of gaiety, gallantry, history, its promises of other places. The scent made something in his heart freshen, as if summer had entered his blood.

Late that afternoon they approached the northwestern edge of the city. He passed the main artery into the interior, and cut off on a boulevard that ran parallel to the water, finally turning into a parking lot alive with memories: the great white convertible, the moon, the sand shimmery with fish. It was a different place now, glinting with hundreds of cars under a merciless sun, filled with the manic noise of human creatures—radios, squalling children, ice-cream vendors—lying like lint over the sound of surf.

He paid the attendant and they drove to the north end of the lot. They checked a row of telephones. They found one that worked and Alice memorized the number. Then he chose a spot on the beach near a breakwater and they laid out a blanket where he would wait.

"You got to promise," she said.

"I did, Alice."

"If I'm not back by seven, I'll call that booth. I'll call it every hour, okay?"

"Sure."

"And you have my number. But nothing's going to happen, is it?"

"Of course not."

"All right," she said, then waved and walked away, the slender body moving with determined clumsy grace. As he watched her leave he was struck by a pang of remorse. It occurred to him Alice was the only one who had ever wanted him for who he was. As if sensing his thought, she turned and ran back, tumbled him into the sand, covered his mouth with hers. He did not resist. He could feel the surreptitious glances as she wiggled over him, her hips pressing in oblivious arousal. When she was breathless she withdrew, without words, her eyes holding his, warning him against betrayal. Then quickly she scampered away. Again he felt a stab of emptiness and started to call out. After a while he got up and went to a beach concession. He ate without tasting. He went to the appointed booth and dialed a number he had memorized long ago, the number the blond woman at the club had given him, belonging to a man he now knew. Perhaps the man had crossed him, hoping to record his arrest, but even if it were so, he felt no particular bitterness. It was this very equanimity that worried him: I shouldn't feel this way, he thought. It's a bad sign.

Before anyone answered, he dropped the receiver back in its cradle, his face flushed with desolation. What could he say to her? And what could she say after leaving and telling Sandzone his whereabouts?

A bitter humming numbed his mind: it was the sound of those other human creatures littering the shore with their clothes too bright and their voices too loud, moving as though they had purpose. He looked at the passersby as if seeing human creatures for the first time: some seemed grotesque, others graced by impossible beauty. Once again he picked up the receiver: after the first ring a recording answered and told him to leave his name and number.

[ 233 ]

"Hello," he said. "This is for Katherine. . . ." He paused, briefly breathless. "It's okay," he said. "Don't feel bad. Whatever happens don't feel bad." There was so much he wanted to say. "Good-bye," he said. Then, not really knowing why, he left the number of the booth.

He bought a pint of whiskey and returned to the blanket, but he did not drink. Instead he wandered restlessly around picking up odd bits of trash and depositing them in an overflowing barrel. There was no discernible anger on his face, only a faint bemused smile. He walked to the water and let a wave break over his feet. He stood staring out at the sea a long time. Then he returned to the blanket and lay back and let the sun take him. He put the harmonica to his lips and breathed softly through the reeds. He played, his eyes closed, a bittersweet music of his own making. Occasionally a bather would stop for a moment and listen. He felt their shadows hover, then move on. But he did not want to see them.

One man stopped for a particularly long time, and seemed to scrutinize Harry, especially the tattoo with its faint scar on his left arm. The man returned with an instant camera and with only a hesitation in stride, took a shot and hurried on. Harry played, oblivious to all but the sun, the water, and the plaint of his own music.

Alice drove up June Street, glancing at the press encampment under the "Welcome Home Alice" banner stretched across the front of the house. The car drew a few casual glances, and a photographer raised a lens, but she was not recognized. She continued around the block and parked on the adjacent street. She sneaked through the side gate into the rear garden of a mock Mediterranean villa, recalling as she ran past the ornately tiled swimming pool how she had almost given in to Mr. Beaumont's eldest son when she was only thirteen. The pool steamed; even in warm weather Mrs. Beaumont kept the heater full up. Everyone around here is even crazier than Harry, Alice thought.

At the southwest corner of the garden she skipped on a series of flagstones across an ornamental pool, then squeezed through a bamboo brake to the wall that separated the Beaumont property from the Fisks'. She gripped the familiar limb of a Chinese elm and swung into the tree, and onto the wall. She was struck by the desolate quiet: the only sound was a high vacant insect murmur. She gazed over the pool to the rear of the house where she had grown up. It looked empty, dead. She took the familiar walk along the wall to another limb and stopped. Go on, she urged herself.

She swung down, landing lightly on all fours, then dashed around the pool to the solarium. The door was unlocked.

There was no one in the living room, and no sound from the kitchen, not even Rosa's television set. But it was Thursday, Rosa's day off. She went upstairs, and peered cautiously into the den where the television set was playing an old movie. There was no one there. She avoided her mother's room, and continued down to her own. When she opened the door she was startled: the wall over her bed was empty. Then she remembered tearing the poster down.

She packed quickly, a few favorite clothes, her passport, a three-month supply of birth-control pills, and her favorite stuffed toy, a small tiger with green glass eyes.

"Good-bye, room," she said.

She listened to a telephone ring three times, then stop. She got up, opened her bedroom window, and stretching as far out as she could, let her suitcase fall.

Marion Fisk was at her makeup table, her face bowed toward her reflection. She shrieked when she glimpsed the shadow of movement. Then she turned, her face pinched between joy and disbelief. For a moment mother and daughter were locked in indecisive stasis, two apparitions, each afraid to acknowledge the other. The trumpeting angels turned in the silence. The Alice's face was buried in the soft lilac-scented shoulder, feeling the awful urge of flesh surround her. O sweet little baby. Sweet sweet poor poor baby. Alice stared numbly over her mother's shoulder, cursing her own tears.

"It's all right," she murmured. "I'm fine. Just fine."

"Oh let me look at you, Alice. Ohh—ohh—" She touched her daughter's face with trembling fingers.

"Where's Daddy?"

Marion Fisk broke into fresh wails. Alice cradled her, and whispered over her shoulder: "Good-bye, Mother," then gently sat the woman down and said with bright cheer: "You wait right here, Mother, and I'll make you a drink. Then I'm going to take a nice long shower, okay?"

She left the water running, and fearing another encounter with her mother, she swung out her bedroom window into the bougainvillea she herself had helped plant a decade before. Oblivious to thorns, in seconds she was on the ground and fleeing the primary scene of babyhood, childhood, and adolescence, fleeing without guilt or regret, she told herself, over the wall past the overheated swimming pool to the little blue sedan. In her urgency to start, she flooded the engine. A wrenching weeping tore her throat. She twisted the key. Please please please, she prayed. The engine sputtered, rolled, died, then suddenly burst into life.

It seemed to take forever to reach the parking lot. As soon as she handed the attendant the bill, she sensed something wrong. The glittering expanse of cars had thinned, and there was a steady stream creeping toward the exit. The attendant seemed to eye her too closely.

"What time is it?" she asked smiling.

Without taking her eyes off her, the attendant said, "Six forty-five."

Pulling away, she stalled. The attendant was still watching her. She parked in the spot nearest the telephone booths. As soon as she got out, she noticed a chromeless beige sedan pull too quickly to the kiosk; the attendant spoke to the driver, then gestured in Alice's direction. She crouched behind a car, and the beige sedan moved to the far end of the lot where there were several others of a similar model. Four or five men, looking too much alike and out of place in ties and sportscoats, were gathered by one of the cars. My god, she thought, what are they doing here? What do they want?

"Is something wrong, miss?" A middle-aged man with a straw hat and Bermuda shorts, a radio in one hand and a can of beer in the other, bowed with a flushed grin. "Nothing wrong, I hope."

"No," she said rising. "Just resting."

She hurried past the phone booths, still looking back over her shoulder. The wind carried scents of charcoal fires and frying meat and a faint tinge of coconut oil. The surf crashed in slow stolid waves. Then something in the light changed; it became diffuse, though still bright; a chill wind brushed goosebumps on her arms. The chill deepened and she began to run toward the jetty, the sand warm under her feet. People stood, gathering blankets around them. The light softened another degree, and her shadow disappeared. The sun was a burning white disk low on the horizon. She stopped and called to him, but she was still a hundred yards away, a freshening breeze blowing against her voice. The first wisps of fog swirled around her, sunstruck apparitions. She slowed, becoming deliberately lackadaisical. She watched the cloudbank a quarter of a mile offshore engulf first one set of sails, then another. A faint bleating of foghorns drifted in between the breaking waves. Around her people laughed with hushed awe, facing the approaching wall of white. She became aware of men moving behind her. She began to run. One of the men began to run too. A jeep appeared, flanking the men. She saw him: he was standing, picking up the blanket when he turned and recognized her. She yelled his name. For a moment he stood immobile, the blanket draped over his shoulder, his shirt at his bare feet. Alice, still running, felt an arm catch her waist and lift her off her feet.

There was no time: there was the hot sand, the chill air, foghorns, yet they stood in bright sun. Sweating men dressed in suits pulled revolvers from under their coats, their ties flapping over their shoulders. One of them yelled at him. The words came forth like chunks of refuse.

The last sound had risen from her throat and died, leaving her breathless. The men walked forward, the jeep still flanking them. Her face burned, her pulse burst in her temples. The fog arrived and simultaneously the brown wool blanket he had held sailed, hung in the air, then collapsed over the man in front. Harry ran. The surf engulfed him. The man fired, then ran into the water, the wave breaking around his feet. He fired into the crashing surf again and again. Then the fog obliterated all.

The wave hit him, rolling him toward the beach, and for an instant he glimpsed the man with the gun. Then he was pulling himself under the next breaking wave. His consciousness was empty, except perhaps for a sensual awareness of the water, its swells and falls, the sound of surf behind him and of the waves shattering over the breakwater before him. Minutes would pass before his tactics in evading his hunters would become conscious and a vision of escape materialize. By that time he had swum past the southern edge of the breakwater, a swell rising him over a submerged rock. He passed close enough to the jetty to see a pair of gulls take off through the fog. The temperature of the water changed. An icy current caught him, sweeping him south. He was beyond any breaking waves, and out here the water was calm, as though having succumbed to the soft feet of the fog. He floated on his back to catch his breath, his eyes closed. Suddenly there was light. He heard splashing nearby. The fog thinned and a bald-headed man with goggles swam toward him with strong mechanical strokes. The man appeared to have been swimming for hours, yet there was no air of fatigue about him. The man nodded to Harry and swam by, then stopped and called back, "You better come in. You can follow me if you like."

"I'll be in in a minute," he said. "I'm okay."

"As you like," the man said. He had a faint indeterminate accent. The fog thickened again and the man disappeared, though Harry could still hear his steady strong strokes.

"Hey," he yelled, but the man was gone. He heard the steady drone of a power launch, moving slowly, and a barrage of foghorns a few hundred yards to the south. Voices passed so close he was sure he could touch the speakers; he heard water lapping against a hull, lush inebriated giggles. A woman blared into a small warning horn, and laughed.

"Sounds like a sick cow."

She was answered by a male voice: "Just keep blowing on that thing."

There followed a hoarse blatting honk, then a shriek of drunken laughter and a few seconds later a wineglass landed beside him, floated a few seconds, then sank. The boat drifted past carrying off the voices, its horn growing fainter. He heard periodic muffled conversation, a distant thrum of engines. He was warm, his body acclimatized to the cold current that carried him. He had lost all sense of direction, but it did not seem to matter.

On the beach a crowd had gathered. Word spread that the kidnapper had been killed. There were a few scattered cheers, intermingled with an equal number of boos. Uniformed forces of the law began to amass in seeming contradiction to the official word of Harold Keller's demise. It was just a question of waiting for the body. The search teams would wait for the fog to break.

Harry had been hearing the bell for what seemed hours before he realized he must have drifted within a few yards of it. He could feel the light change behind the fog. He reached out and touched the buoy. The fog broke and he was dazzled by the sun, a fiery ball sinking beneath the swells. He clung to the rocking clanging buoy, and watched the wall of fog move onto the land.

Then it was dark. He saw moving lights. A helicopter

hammered over, flashing a searchlight across the water to the north. He did not remember letting go of the buoy, he simply realized he no longer heard the bell. He floated on his back, without orientation, aware only of the immensity of water, the great flux pulling him. And without thought, he released himself to the arms of the water, until he no longer knew where he ended and water began. He was immersed in a medium, warm and serene. *I wish . . . I wish . . .*

*and all was flowing flowing*
*feet in muddy waters*
*the sky     blue and always*
*the rustling cottonwoods speaking to the raft . . .*
*then the change:*
*leaf smoke*
*and sky cold*
*big*
*white*
*the river slows     freezes     and on the snowswept ice*
*we moved*
*under the circle of colored lights*
*behind the little clouds of our breath*
*our smiles     unafraid     in random parade*
*around the fire . . .*

He began to laugh: the laughter seemed to rise from deep within, perhaps from beyond himself, from the water that carried him. He yearned to share this laughter, but he was alone, a human creature taken by the tide. His laughter finally expended itself in tears, but these were tears he had never experienced before: he had the sensation these tears were the ocean itself weeping through him.

He had no idea how long he had been in the water. If someone had informed him it had been almost eight hours, he would have scoffed. Then he saw lights twinkling in the distance. It was the curse of human creatures to build, to dream. They would forever be trying to make their lights in the darkness. It was laughable. Yet oddly touching. He had to admire it, even for all its foolishness. He felt the call of the distant lamps. Am I dreaming? he thought. Am I alive?

The lamplight was far and blurry in his eyes, but he began to reach for it. It was almost a duty to return. And with his acknowledgment of the lights, he experienced fear. Perhaps they would be waiting to punish him. The others with their laws, their blueprints for how life was to be lived. But somehow the fear no longer consumed him. There was something in him larger than his fear, something unnameable and fierce—a heartbeat he could identify as earned, his own, reaching for the twinkling lights on the beach.